Praise for Different Kinds of Defiance

"DIFFERENT KINDS OF DEFIANCE is a collection of stories that are both tender and explosive, centering resistance towards bleak futures and inaction, collaboration and community, restoration, social justice, environmental impact, and rebellions and risked lives aimed at reparations all told through musical prose written by an experienced hand and polished voice. Bernardo effectively subverts stereotypes and redefines concepts. These stories plant seeds of hope for the future and caution us against what humanity stands to both gain and lose as a result of technology, science, and most of all human-centric thinking."

—Ai Jiang, Nebula Finalist and author of LINGHUN and I AM AI

· · · · ● · ● · · · ·

"In DIFFERENT KINDS OF DEFIANCE, Renan Bernardo highlights the best of humanity against the backdrop of a world destroyed by humans. These stories are full of emotion and spirit, and are absolutely delightful."

—Lesley Conner, editor-in-chief of Apex Magazine

· · · ● · ● · ◐ · · · ·

"In DIFFERENT KINDS OF DEFIANCE, Bernado pulls off a feat of **fierce and riveting storytelling**, with a glimpse of a world that is at once torn and ravaged, yet full of hope. It's no baseless reassurance, but a call for the hard work to be done, to hold on to what we love. From pushing back against damage in "A Shoreline of Oil and Infinity," to the unlikely alliances and innovation of "Eight Steps to Steal a Yacht and Build and Hospital," and the ways our lives and love adapt in "When It's Time to Harvest." While the geek in me enjoyed the technical details of the tatuí bots and the organisation structure of the farming collectives, DkD is more than just parables for a sustainable future. It's **a brilliant picture of resilience, and a promise that we can and will do better**."

—Eliane Boey, author of OTHER MINDS and CLUB CONTANGO

· · · · ● · ● · · · ·

"DIFFERENT KINDS OF DEFIANCE offers heart-rending and moving stories of small miracles. In Renan Bernardo's world, miracles aren't the deeds of saints, but of everyday people who count on themselves and each other for survival against a harsh landscape."

—Eugenia Triantafyllou, Ignyte, Nebula and World Fantasy

Award-finalist author

· · · ● · ● · ● · · ·

"Step into a vibrant yet vulnerable future reimagined in Renan Bernardo's DIFFERENT KINDS OF DEFIANCE, where solarpunk visions meet the harsh realities of climate change, weaving human drama of resilience and innovation in a world transformed by environmental challenges."

—Chen Qiufan, author of WASTE TIDE and co-author of AI2041: TEN VISIONS FOR OUR FUTURE

· · · ● · ● · ● · · ·

"The ten stories of DIFFERENT KINDS OF DEFIANCE are fiercely hopeful and ready to fight for something better. Bernardo's characters are full of heart as well as defiance. I'd gladly have read ten more like this, and I can't wait to see what he brings us next."

—Marissa Lingen

Different Kinds of Defiance

Renan Bernardo

Android Press

"Eight Steps to Steal a Yacht and Build a Hospital" was originally published in *Solarpunk Magazine #8*.

"A Shoreline of Oil and Infinity" was originally published in *Escape Pod #863*.

"Soil of Our Home, Storm of Our Lives" was originally published in *Apex Magazine #128*.

"Anticipation of Hollowness" was originally published in *World Science Fiction #2 – Reloading the Future*.

"When It's Time to Harvest" was originally published in *Imagine 2200 - Climate Fiction for Future Ancestors* (2021).

"Even Though You're No More" was originally published in *Three Crows Magazine #8*.

"Look to the Sky, My Love" was originally published in *Solarpunk Magazine #1*.

"The River That Passed Through My Life" was originally published in Portuguese by Editora Dame Blanche.

Thank you to New Press for the waiving of exclusive publication rights to "When It's Time to Harvest" so it could appear in this collection.

Published by Android Press
Eugene, Oregon
www.android-press.com

ISBN: 978-1958121771

Contents

Introduction

Rioverse

So, what is the Rioverse? In a nutshell, it's a version of Rio de Janeiro where the ocean levels rose dramatically due to the unattended consequences of climate change. A series of climate catastrophes disrupted governments all around as the consequence of a chain of bad decisions. In the end, the wealthy and the lucky were able to flee to seasteads, higher grounds, and cities far from the coasts. But our current climate crisis doesn't threaten only coastal cities. It threatens the very fabric of democracies, the way we live, and how the world functions in general. So, when all "turnarounds" failed, the rich went to the Dandelions, 104 space modules orbiting the Earth—a solution devised to actually "replace" the need for a planet. It's an extreme scenario, and rather unlikely in the real world, but one that nevertheless lingers in the minds of billionaires all the time. You can read more about the Dandelions and how they were projected in "The River That Passed Through My Life," the novelette that closes this collection.

The idea of a Rioverse came years ago, when I read a piece of news in *The Guardian* about what would happen with some cities (Miami, Osaka, Shanghai, and Rio among them) if the average temperature in the world went up only 3C. People forget that the rise of sea levels isn't only tied to the melting of glaciers and ice sheets, but also to thermal expansion: in higher temperatures, the fundamental particles get more energetic and excited, and water occupies more space. In the article, there was a map of Rio with a simulation of how the city would look like if the water levels rose dramatically, with the ocean forcing its veins through the streets, fusing with lagoons and lakes, blurring the coastlines, and changing its map. It was inevitable to think about how people would survive in this version of Rio.

Despite its post-apocalyptical nature, the Rioverse is also a place full of hope. It can be seen in all three stories in this collection, but perhaps specially in "When It's Time to Harvest," set a bit further into the future than the other two. I like to describe the Rioverse as post-apocalyptical moving to Solarpunk and perhaps aiming for utopia at some point in the future. So, despite all the chaos and struggle inherent to a world shook by a severe climate crisis, you'll surely find hope, fight, and life all around, mainly in the characters inhabiting this future Rio (and hopefully never to be real).

I have four stories in this world, three of which are in this collection and the other one unpublished. I also have plans to write more stories set in the Rioverse. So, you'll hopefully embark on another adventure soon enough.

EIGHT STEPS TO STEAL A YACHT AND BUILD A HOSPITAL

The first story in the collection is set in the Rioverse. I picked this story to open the anthology because it's a more fast-paced, kind of action-packed story, but also because it brings together a lot of Solarpunk and Climate Fiction elements that I deem important: cooperatives, food distribution, and healthcare in places impacted by the climate crisis; resilience of minorities; life in a profoundly changed urban environment; social collapse; resilient applications of technology; reclamation of the public space; and non-tolerance to groups based on hate.

What I tried to achieve with this story was to show a Rio de Janeiro severely struggling with the rise in the level of the oceans and the overall degradation of the city, but containing a lot of communities strong enough to unite, make a difference, and to make the city livable. This is shown in the Trepadeira Hospital-Farm co-op, but also in all of the main characters (Hamilton, Monique, and Alex). I'd also wanted to introduce some solutions to problems that are aggravated in the Rio of the story, but that are also problems nowadays: the reach of a functioning healthcare system (including the access to gender confirmation surgery), food distribution (slightly shown in the form of the vertical farm and Alex), organ donation and transplantation, and the striking difference between the wealthy and those who barely make a living.

Men like Fraj0linha are well known both here in Brazil and worldwide: far right, wealthy people who only care about themselves and vouch for a fake illusion of traditionalism. I tried to show his conservative side through his illusive support of a Brazilian Monarchy comeback. Sadly, this is a real, far right movement in Brazil (fortunately verging on irrelevance, though it acquired a bunch of followers in the last few years). I tried to convey the idea that even in the future these movements might still exist, but mainly that they can be fought and resisted.

· · · · **·** · **·** · · **·** · ·

1. Stealing a yacht

How naive of Hamilton to think stealing would be the hardest part of his plan. Not to say that his belly doesn't flutter with anxiety as he waits for Alex. After all, it's the first time he's stealing—looting first aid kits and medical equipment isn't stealing. But what he's doing is for a good cause, he tells himself over and over.

"It is," he says out loud as if that'll make it truer. He's sitting on a dock that juts out of the window of a deteriorated building. All around him, other flaking, overly-patched buildings cast shadows along the floodstreet. The lucky ones surviving above the waterline.

Sweat drips from Hamilton's flimsy beard. The day is scorching—what day isn't in Rio de Janeiro, right?—but his agitation has a part to play in it too. The floodstreet is empty except for a boy rowing with a drone buzzing at his side. Alex should be there by now, along with the muscle from Trepadeira Vertical Farm he promised would come to help with the theft. But he isn't. How can you hope to pull off a crime if you can't even keep an eye on the clock?

Hamilton has visuals on the PatriotiKat. The 98-meter, white-hulled, five-decked yacht is parked exactly where a luxury sports car would have been parked a century ago, perhaps situated in front of a clubhouse or, most likely, merely placed as a showoff to passersby. But the yacht is meters above the old street level, softly swaying along with the littered, miry tide. Leblon, once a wealthy neighborhood, is out of fashion. It's now a bay of rooftop islets, lichen-embraced buildings, and lone treasure seekers.

Another thing out of fashion is rich, far-right influencers. Fraj0linha, a weapons aficionado and the yacht's owner, has lost its precious boat in a set of fuzzy bureaucratic proceedings devised by Alex. All Fraj0linha wanted was a complete, high-quality hulljob—cleaning, painting, dry blasting, antifouling—which Alex promised to provide in his small dummy corp, all prettified to attract easy money.

"You okay with it, *garotão*?"

Hamilton turns back, staring up at the bulky man standing behind him on the dock. Alex is wearing his usual suspenders, smudgy with the Trepadeira's fertilizer and dirt. Must've been dealing with the gourds and cauliflowers that the Trepadeira yield this time of year. His mustache is misaligned on his face due to a scar on his left cheek.

"You came alone?" Hamilton asks, squinting at the building's window to see if there's anyone else there.

Alex snorts. "C'mon, garotão. That thing is already stolen. It's only a matter of sailing it back to the hospital."

Hamilton's eyes widen. It can't be that easy. In his worst nightmares, he'd depicted gunfights, ambushes, blood—even his own—reddening the floodstreets. He overanalyzed it multiple times, knowing he'd eventually convince himself to go on without feeling guilty. He's doing it for Monique, he keeps telling himself. For her and for everyone that goes through the same things they went through years ago, in the Day. He and Monique had to dash through the Atlantic-poked floodstreets in an autoboat toward a faraway clinic where she could have her liver transplanted in an emergency unit. At the time, he was a woman with a name amazingly out of place, and Monique was only a friend. Now his body and name fit into him, and Monique is his dear wife.

And that yacht over there, lined up with photovoltaic cells along with its five decks, will be his way of bringing health where it's virtually unavailable. His revenge against the Day.

"You okay with what we're gonna do, boy?" Alex says. "Stealing from that *babaquinha* is totally fine by me, but I'm not sure if you're gonna sleep at night."

Hamilton pinches his lips. Most certainly he won't sleep for a while. But Alex doesn't need to know that. He nods firmly, trying to convey he's fine with stealing the yacht.

Monique, on the other hand, won't be. She is the head doctor at Jerônimo General Hospital, the place where they've worked and lived for almost ten years—another of the good things that came after the Day. He's a nurse, even though everything he learned of the trade was by reading books and seeing other people doing the job. But that's how it is these days, right? Better to have an unskilled, non-graduated nurse than no nurse at all.

Alex fetches a crude wooden canoe from the building and slops it on the water. They row to the PatriotiKat. The hull really needs a paint job, and it's easy to understand why Fraj0linha trusted it in the hands of one of the seemingly outstanding companies Alex devised for his thefts. Near the waterline, the boat is pockmarked by Rio's brackish mix of lichen and mud, scratched by the barrage of debris and trash the shiny yacht must've found in its path. But all the other aspects of the boat scream "Hey, look at me, I'm completely out of place here in this dingy floodstreet." Out of time as well, since a Brazilian Monarchy flag some 260 years obsolete waves over the bridge. On the hull, a kooky, black-and-white cat with red eyes and green paws clings clumsily to a heavy machine gun. Fraj0linha's mascot, a paragon of bad taste.

As they climb the rope ladder to the PatriotiKat, Hamilton's body shivers all throughout. But that's part of the package that comes with this enterprise: sweat, fear, second guesses, and the implacable desire to jump and swim away from that thing.

"Relax, boy. We do a lot of these man-in-the-middle cons." Alex laughs, barging into the cockpit as if it's his bedroom. "We get a lot of stuff from the gated condos in Barra. Sometimes they don't even notice. We skim the lists of things they're trying to sell or repair, pose as potential service providers, get them to put what we want where we want it... doesn't always work, but when it does..." He slides a hand over the varnished wheel and kisses the tips of his fingers.

"And now we just..." Hamilton smiles lamely.

"Turn it on and sail back. We've overridden their security bots and any active trackers. Everything else was already turned off 'for repairs'." Alex laughs. "There's a small risk someone might see us sailing this toy. But once we hide it in the harbor and give it a refurbishment... then we're mostly safe. In a week or so it will be just one more yacht salvaged from an abandoned marina a decade ago."

Hamilton gulps and nods. He reminds himself it's for Monique. It's for his dear wife who puts her soul on the line to maintain the Jerônimo every single day. When they transform that gaudy colossus into a moving hospital, people wouldn't have to die at home, unreachable for treatment. They wouldn't perish giving birth as though they were living in the Dark Ages of Rio, desperately sailing around to reach poorly-equipped hospitals or clinics. They wouldn't agonize through completely treatable diseases or live in bodies they don't feel comfortable with. They wouldn't suffer as Monique had, in need of a liver.

"Alex?" His voice is suddenly too loud in the cabin. He cringes and almost whispers the next words, "Don't tell Monique, please."

"Wouldn't even dream about it, garotão."

Two catamarans join them on the way to the Jerônimo—heavily-armed farm friends from Alex. Just in case.

All the while, Hamilton keeps his teeth clenched and his hands gripping the stern's railing. But, yes, despite the knot in the pit of his stomach, there's also a drop—or a few—of hope somewhere within him. They're going to do it. They're doing it.

This leads us to the next step.

2. Lying to your loved one about the yacht in the harbor

And that's harder than part one. Hamilton was never good at lying to Monique, to begin with.

He proposed to her many months before the Day, deciding they needed a beautiful view for that moment, something special to remember. Sunlight glistening on the flood-streets, seagulls showing off their flying skills over neglected buildings, the abandoned seasteads like distant monuments off the coast. A romantic post-collapse date, right? Besides, looking at Rio from up high was always a good way to obscure its problems and muffle your own. So Hamilton led Monique to one of the old trails leading to Vista Chinesa. The high ground where the lookout was located had been mostly spared by the waters, so they spent four hours going up, indulging themselves in the luxury of getting their legs tired. It was perfect. Monique said yes and they spent the night in an abandoned cottage nearby. But of course, Monique knew what he was planning all along. No one went to Vista Chinesa anymore, if not for something special.

But, well... It's another kind of lying to tell your wife the yacht in the harbor is perfectly legitimate. It's not the kind of lie that could bloom into something cute and exhilarating like a proposal underneath starlight. It's more about hiding something from plain sight, like all the stuff lost underwater over the years. And like those rotten things, this kind of lie is just waiting to be fished out.

"Alex found it lying around," Hamilton tells her, not unaware of the weight in his chest. "At Leblon." They're in their suite on the hospital's top floor, looking over the harbor between the Jerônimo and the Trepadeira, which Alex calls the backbone of the hospital-farm co-op.

"Lying around? A yacht like that is not a half-sunk barge one finds spoiled in floodstreet docks." She's exhausted. Though the flux of patients on the Jerônimo isn't huge, they're always understaffed. The fatigue is clear on the jagged lines of her cheeks and the way she forgot to remove her shoes after her shift. She'd just removed her white coat and her shirt. Hamilton wished she'd forgotten to kiss him too--it would make him feel less guilty. But she didn't. Kisses always taste sour on the lips of the liar.

"It belonged to some influencer years ago... I think... The yacht was just there to be claimed. It will take a while to adapt it, but it's exactly what we need for the mobile hospital. We'll need proper medical equipment, of course. Bioreactors for harvesting organs and tissues, MRI scanners, stuff for at least one operating room... All in due time."

"Guess sometimes we're lucky... We need to find a nice gift

for Alex." Monique touches the window and leans her head on it. She's not looking at him, but she sees her half-smile reflected in the window. Hamilton scans the J-shaped incision on her torso. That's the most visible mark the Day left on her, but there are many others, unseen, shrouded by the busy life she now lives on the Jerônimo. Hamilton often wonders whether Monique knows how close to dying she'd been on the Day. He'd never had the guts to ask.

"What's happening in here?" Monique knocks on his forehead. He traces his finger on her scar, and though he remembers the laughter when they married on a rooftop and Alex decided to play the violin, what really inundates his mind are Monique's lips quivering, her nails tearing his palm as he fumbled with the controls of an autoboat, hoping 150km wasn't that far, cursing himself for his incompatible liver.

"How I'd do anything for you." He softly touches her arms and kisses her mouth.

That's not a lie, no. Hamilton would really do anything for Monique. But after you tell a lie to someone you love, every other word that leaves your mouth feels smudged with falseness.

3. Erasing the influencer

This part is supposed to be easy. Alex convenes fifteen of his most trustworthy Trepadeira farmers and three personal friends, while Hamilton calls a few people from the hospital staff. In less than twenty-four hours, they manage to seal the swimming pool in the first deck above the waterline, remove all summer party paraphernalia, paint over the helipad, and set aside Fraj0linha's deactivated drones for reprogramming.

The next step is erasing the red-eyed, green-pawed, weaponized cat from the hull. It's kind of cathartic to see it vanishing. They apply loads of industrial solvent on it, rub power sand to eradicate the signs of Fraj0linha, then the primer and the polyurethane paint. Hamilton thinks about adding a red stripe along the hull to indicate the boat's new medical function. Or perhaps a red cross? And how would it be called from now on? He leaves those decisions for later. The right thing to do would be to ask Monique's opinion as he always did with anything regarding the Jerônimo.

"The external job is almost done, *garotão*," Alex yells from the second deck, signaling quickly to a woman in a smaller motor boat anchored a few decks from the yacht. She gives him a thumbs up. Alex has set up a security team along the harbor in strategic positions at the hospital, on the farm rooftops, and in the floodstreets around the co-op. *I'm only a brute lettuce puller*, Alex uses to say. *But one day I'll be head of security of all the Rio co-ops.*

The yacht's inner parts will need much more meticulous work. They'd need to completely refurbish the dozens of cabins and galleries, stripping them of their luxury and replacing them with medical equipment, infirmaries, and at least one ICU. Some things they could bring from the hospital, but others would need to be acquired elsewhere. That would be the work of months, but they agreed on a minimum operating capacity that would enable the boat—calling it a yacht doesn't fit anymore!—to traverse the waters of Rio and bring health wherever it's needed.

But, as you've read above: This part is supposed to be easy. Well, it is... for the boat. Not for Hamilton. You must be thinking: "oh no, Fraj0linha's lackeys found them and will break into the harbor with guns blazing!" That's not the case, fortunately.

What happens is that Monique is no fool. As soon as the unusual fuss in the harbor annoyed some of the inpatients, she decided to check it out. When she arrives on the yacht's dock in her white coat, a stethoscope around her neck, terracotta lipstick slightly smudged on her lower lip, Hamilton knows he's in trouble.

"Why all the security?" she asks, squinting at the disappearing cat on the boat's hull.

"It's stolen." Hamilton bursts it out. He can't lie to her, no matter what. "I'm sorry..."

Of all the reactions he expects from his wife—those born of anger, incredulity, and disappointment—crying isn't one of them.

4. Regaining your loved one's trust

If you've betrayed your lover's trust, you know how it might be hard to gain it back. That's why Hamilton stops abruptly when he finds Monique in the hospital cafeteria that night, sitting alone, slightly stooped forward. A cup of black coffee rests on the table, barely touched, with a pillbox of immunosuppressants next to it.

When the waters came, slowly but surely, Rio was already drenched in a severe economical and humanitarian crisis caused by a mostly ignored climate crisis. Many had already fled to safer grounds distant from coastlines, and most of the wealthy had relocated to seasteads and space stations. Health services in Rio took a major blow. Hospitals shut down, others were ransacked, or seized by paramilitary groups, fake governments, or milicianos. Rio's health system became a scattered web of professionals and amateurs, many without degrees or proper knowledge, distributed over field hospitals, clandestine clinics, and just a few official places that the Brazilian government and its public universities strived to maintain.

Enter Monique, a doctor, his wife. When she came back to the Jerônimo, she arrived with the desire to link the islands of healthcare that inevitably came with the breakdown of government and the formation of floodstreets. But with the years, the realization that she couldn't do more than she was already doing dawned on her, sapping her energy and hope. That's where Hamilton thinks he fits, and that's one of the reasons he came up with the plan for stealing the yacht. If he could at least pave the road for Monique's ambitions, he'd be happy.

Hamilton enters the cafeteria, slowly, not wanting to draw attention lest anyone see the guilt dribbling from him.

"Hey," he says, pinching his lips, approaching Monique, but not being a fool to sit uninvited. Not now. Perhaps she didn't want him there at all.

Monique nods at him. She's been crying again. The lipstick is still smudged on her lip and Hamilton knows exactly how it would taste on his lips. Strawberry and disappointment.

"He's a bad person," Hamilton blurts out.

"Who?"

"The influencer. A self-declared monarchist and an alt-right maniac."

Hamilton slides his pad over the table. It plays a video

loop of Fraj0linha laughing while some of his friends shoot at a half-collapsed building with people trying to desperately flee.

Monique closes her eyes, pushes the pad away, and grabs the box of immunosuppressants. She'd need them for the rest of her life. She might even need another liver transplant at some point. Hamilton feels dizzy with the sudden thought of another transplant.

"I don't want to see this kind of video now," she says. "I know people like him exist. It's only that…"

Hamilton sits in front of her. Uninvited, fine. A drone swirls by in the air, scanning them in case they want to order something. One of the toys Alex's farmers scavenged from an abandoned office building downtown.

"You're afraid for the co-op…" Hamilton says. "And for us."

Monique nods, squeezing her wrists. She'd helped deliver five babies today.

"This video… It just reinforces my point. What if this influencer comes by shooting at us?"

"His yacht will be unrecognizable. It almost is right now. You've seen what we're doing."

"Doesn't matter." She shrugs. "It's no guarantee of anything. Co-ops need protection and safety. Alex says it all the time. I… I'm not against stealing from that craphead influencer. Hell, he probably stole it himself, right? And the fact that it can help us bring health to more people is great. But…"

The Jerônimo-Trepadeira co-op—or the pill-lettuce friendship as Alex puts it—had been an obvious union. On one side, Monique started managing the abandoned hospital where she already worked before the collapse. On the other,

Alex Magalhães, a former mechanic, decided to grow food for his friends and family, an undertaking that evolved to be an important vertical farm in the Olaria neighborhood. And now Hamilton, who didn't struggle half as much as Monique had to resuscitate a half-drowned hospital, is jeopardizing it all because he decided to steal from a childish boy.

"I'll tell Alex to take it away from here," he says, letting his breath out. "Tomorrow morning."

Monique puts a hand over his, her eyes suddenly focusing on him. "I'll speak with Alex to bring some hands from the co-op of community cops. If this boat reaches where healthcare is virtually non-existent... Then I think it's worth the risk."

Hamilton gulps, staring down at his hands on his lap. For a moment, he was completely convinced by what Monique said about their safety. *Caramba*, he was practically co-opted by her argument to the point of wanting to get rid of the yacht right away. And he would've kept that opinion, but he recalls Monique's nails sinking hard on his palm, drawing blood from it while they sailed away toward the only place where she could be saved.

Monique pulls his chin up with a finger.

"And, *meu amor*..." She manages to find a smile somewhere. "Don't lie to me again. You know you can't."

5. Finding bioreactors

For that, Hamilton picks the ancient, partially collapsed and submerged Hospital do Fundão. Once a thriving university hospital, then a refugee hub, now the place is set of cavernous corridors reeking of mold and sewage, barely echoing its past. What his sources in the Jerônimo told him is that there's a lab room with a set of five apparently functioning bioreactors adapted for organ and limb growth. So that's his bet. Five is enough for the Saúdiate basic operation. (He's been calling it Saúdiate, a portmanteau of "health" and "yacht.")

He points his flashlight ahead and peeks at his pad. Turn right, then left, then up the stairs. He could've brought some of Alex's friends, but he didn't want to draw attention. He wore his worst clothes—you could safely call them rags—and decided to check if the bioreactors were still there. If they were, they could come back later with a knowledgeable team to move the equipment without damaging it—and fetch whatever else they needed for the Jerônimo. These sorts of scouting operations are how they usually restock the co-op.

The lab room is open, its door long gone. A damp draft swooshes out from it. The sunlight that penetrates the building's many crevices illuminates particles of dust in the air.

Ah! Olha vocês aí! The five bioreactors are in place, all set in a row. They appear intact and untouched, a forgotten picture of a gone world, framed by dust and darkness. He would need only to—

His pad clangs its emergency tone across the deserted lab. Alex.

His first thought is Fraj0linha. He touches the screen to accept the call.

"Alex, what's up?"

"It's Monique..."

6. Regretting your decisions as you sail back to the place where you saved a lot of people to try and save the one you love

This is the easy part, unfortunately. When regret comes, it comes at high speed.

Monique's acute liver failure is a time bomb. They both could see the timer ticking, ticking, ticking... When still a kid, Monique suffered a blood clot in the hepatic artery, which progressively damaged her liver throughout the years. She always planned to do something about it, but when her parents died in a flood and the city of Rio was officially broken and drowned in chaos, she had no other option but to postpone it. By then, the Atlantic Ocean had "only" claimed ten meters of the street level, but most of the urban mobility was already done by means of boats. Hamilton and Monique managed to rebuild a sketch of their lives in that new, wetter way of life, slowly reigniting whatever plans they could.

They'd already been discussing how she'd undergo the surgical revascularization she needed when, one morning, Monique woke up screaming and struggling. The Day had started, at a time when Rio's citizens had been accumulating their own personal and inevitable Days. Hamilton had already planned a few things in case of emergencies. The number of donors and lab-grown organs was especially low in Rio for many years, but after the complete collapse, organ transplants became almost a myth. Luckily—if anything in those circumstances could be considered luck—a group of Caribbean refugees had developed an app that scanned hospitals and clinics with organs available for transplants. Hamilton kept it right on his pad's main screen, at a finger's reach.

When the time bomb went off, he washed painkillers down Monique's throat, got his landlord's autoboat, and guided it through the floodstreets and into a hospital out of the city. It was the only one that showed a green, hopeful icon for a healthy lab-grown liver. That would be Monique's only shot at living, he knew as he reconfigured the boat's algorithms to boost through its max speed. The fact Monique arrived at dry land alive was a miracle. The fact they managed to quickly hitch a ride at the back of a truck was another miracle. And the fact that the transplant was ultimately a success was the last miracle of the longest day of their lives.

As Hamilton speeds a Jerônimo's autoboat along the extended coast of Guanabara Bay, all he remembers are Monique's wails, her nails pressing deeply into his skin, her breath, ragged and weighty, and the merciless scorching sun glistening its light on the beads of sweat on her brow. He clicks his teeth and blinks fast, trying to focus on something else. Half-drowned buildings skitter by his sides, bare glimpses of damp concrete.

A few months after the Day, they married, something they've been postponing as well, the memories of the Vista Chinesa proposal now dully mixed with all the things that happened after. About the same time, Hamilton started the hormone therapy and Monique came back to the Jerônimo, where she'd worked after her graduation, and planned to resume its operation. Hamilton tries to focus on those things, good things, healthy things, bred of love and care, but they quickly drain from his mind, replaced by Alex's words on the pad call.

She disappeared, man. Someone posing as a patient came by and... They took her, man. And they left a warning. The damned influencer wants his yacht back in 24 hours or...

Hamilton hung up on him. He knew his next words and he didn't want to hear them. Another thing he knew was how reckless he was for stealing the yacht. He'd put his life on the line, but most of all, if anyone traced the theft back to the co-op, everybody else's lives were on the line too, including the head doctor's. That's as simple as a basic sum, and yet it only comes to him now, like a nagging thought drilling through the corners of his mind. As if it's not too late. What makes it all worse is that there's no guarantee that Fraj0linha won't kill Monique after he has his yacht back. For a man who posts videos hanging people in the name of the rightful King of Brazil, killing someone would be completely within character.

Gripping tight the boat's wheel—needlessly, since it's following its algorithms—Hamilton taps his pad to call Alex.

"It's simple, isn't it?" He says before Alex can utter a word. "It has to be."

"Giving back the yacht and getting Monique back?" The fact that Alex's voice is rough and without any of his usual humor is bad. "Negotiation is the standard procedure in those cases, but... We can't trust these extremist leftovers from the beginning of the century, Hamilton."

"You said it was safe..." Blaming someone for your own decisions. Great. That's what Hamilton is thinking as his autoboat swerves right and dashes through a floodstreet flanked by rooftop islets sporting shacks and huts of exposed brick.

"I said there was a small risk. We weren't tracked by any devices. The farm folks had stripped the yacht of its electronic stuff and deactivated all possible trackers. But... one of his thousands of followers must've spotted us between

Leblon and the co-op harbor. We were unlucky... Trust me, Hamilton, I'd never go on with your plan if I thought the risk was big. You know me."

Hamilton grits his teeth. Of all risks, the smallest is the one that comes right back at him like a dreadful piranha hopping out of the water. Working as a nurse, he's well aware of what risk management means. It's always painful and terrifying to take something from one patient and give it to another. You have to hope it's only temporary suffering, as you ask for another nurse to find an oxygen tank, more serum, painkillers, or antibiotics that aren't expired... And on the Day, when he enveloped a desperate Monique in his arms and kissed her forehead, he knew the world was against him. Death. That was how the Day would end. He was sure of it. How could he get Monique across a crumbling city and still hope for her to endure liver transplantation? People died from far less than that.

"Alex..." he whispers.

"Yes?"

"Did she bring her medicines? She needs them. My God... That can't be happening."

"I don't know, man."

By now, clinging to the flimsy thoughts about his marriage and his hormone therapy seems like distant foolishness.

7. Rescuing your loved one before she's killed (it's all your fault, yes, it is, you shouldn't have kickstarted this plan)

That's how things work, isn't it? You have step-by-step instructions you aim to follow in order to accomplish something. But then, along the way, you make a mistake and it all falls apart, so you desperately pick up the fragments of your initial plans amidst the turmoil you caused. You need to set it all back in order, through gritted teeth, tears, and frustration.

Fraj0linha has set up a point off the coast for the negotiations, roughly where the old Copacabana Beach used to be. The choice is obvious—and appalling—enough: Shootouts and executions off the coast don't draw as much attention as ones that happen in the floodstreets.

The co-op sends seven small tug boats to escort the yacht and provide protection during the negotiation. Aboard is a party of volunteers gathered by Alex: farmers, nurses, doctors, and a detachment from the community cops co-op. Much of the influencer's stuff had been brought back to the yacht to avoid further reasons to displease the man. But some things would have to stay unchanged. Like the hateful cat, now absent from the hull, and the x-ray and MRI machines already installed in a few cabins. Has to be enough.

The negotiation is to happen on the yacht's pool deck, the first one above the waterline, as per Fraj0linha's instructions (whoever holds a life in their hand gives the orders). The influencer and eight of his minions arrive in a motorboat and as soon as the boats bump, a man ties a rope to the yacht as if leashing a dog.

Alex tries to insist that Hamilton stay in one of the tugboats, but Hamilton would never flee from the responsibility of righting the things he messed up. He touches his shirt pocket and feels Monique's immunosuppressant pillbox in it. This relieves him somehow as if a part of her is still there with him. But when he actually sees Monique, brought onto the deck by Fraj0linha's minions, his heart misses more than a beat. She's tied with ropes around on a chaise lounge, still wearing her white coat and her working, slightly battered shoes. She's gagged and a strip of blood runs from her left cheek. But she's alive, eyes alert and relieved to see the co-op folks coming aboard.

The influencer is taller than he seems on his videos, but the grin he usually sports when he's vomiting his crap online is now replaced by worry-carved dimples on a stubbled face with the paleness timidly replaced by the tan of Rio. He wears a sleeveless shirt with a Brazilian flag crowned with a Monarchy crest. One of the men—shirtless, a map of scars charted on his belly—holds a submachine gun and sticks to the influencer's side like a father afraid to leave his son. By the look in his eyes, he's paid—and highly so—to keep that stance.

The first thing Hamilton does is look straight into the barrel of the gun. That's because he steps forward and extends the pillbox to Monique.

"Please," he mutters, dead coldness on his brow. "It's just her medicine. She should've taken it a while ago."

"Throw it away, José," Fraj0linha says, a curl of disgust on his face. José, the shirtless bodyguard, rips the box from Hamilton's hand, but instead of throwing it over the gunwale, he sticks it into his trousers. You don't just throw things away like that. Good choice, José.

"It will all be simple," Alex says, but it sounds as if he's trying to convince himself. And he is. He took the role of mediator, so he's not armed. "We leave with her. You and your men stay in the yacht."

Fraj0linha squints at Alex. Hamilton steps back and joins

the other co-op folks, his gaze latched on Monique. He breathes deeply, finally able to find some slivers of hope in that mess. First, it wouldn't take long. In minutes, he'd be embracing and kissing his wife, saying he's sorry and promising he would never do anything like that again. Second, since Fraj0linha came aboard, the negotiation isn't likely to end in a bloodbath. Stories from the start of the century often described alt-right extremists valuing life above everything. But only one: Their own. Fraj0linha wouldn't risk his precious, pale skin in a shootout to kill a bunch of farmers and nurses.

"You're dirty," Fraj0linha says, his eyes on Alex. "You're all like... You know the trash that clogs up around the corners of some floodstreets? You're like that. And you stink of... earth?"

Alex sniffs his armpit. "Today it's turnips, I think."

"You deceived me, pobretão," Fraj0linha bites his lips, apparently finding some pleasure in calling Alex a penniless man. "José told me you were very smart with that phony repairs company."

"We thought we could borrow the yacht for some community work." It's Hamilton who says that. Not Alex, not any of the other co-op folks. So, kudos for his sudden courage. "But we have no problem giving it back to you. We're sorry for the inconvenience and desire you no harm."

"Community work?" Fraj0linha snorts. "Like what?"

"Healthcare, my liege," José says. "We found some hospital equipment in the cabins. They're from the Jerônimo-Trepadeira co-op in Olaria."

"Healthcare?" Fraj0linha laughs. "Do you call those filthy clinics in those wobbly buildings healthcare? I have true healthcare in my condo, with doctors who graduated from the United States' best universities."

"We thought we could help folks with a boat like that..." Hamilton says, but his voice is feeble, his arms and legs trembling. "There are many people who need it."

"Blah-blah-blah... Kill them."

"Wait!" Alex yells. On the chaise lounge, Monique groans and widens her eyes. Hamilton, on the other hand, doesn't move. Not because he can't, but because of something he sees. A thread lost in the web of José's scars.

Fraj0linha leaps back into his motorboat, which quickly gains distance from the yacht (the king is always the first to get to safety, right?). His minions, led by José, point their submachine guns and pistols at the co-op folks, one for each, except for Monique, who is already utterly defenseless.

There are things you can only do when you're on the edge. In those moments, the world shuts all around you and only one thing matters. Hyperfocus, doctors call it. On the Day, that thing was Monique, moaning, unable to form words, growling out her pain across the floodstreets. And Hamilton poured all his attention and strength and thoughts onto her. So he could program the autoboat's algorithms to go North, leaving Rio behind; so he could carry her for a kilometer across a barren road until they found a bottled water truck going to someplace near the clinic where the liver was waiting for her; so he could cry alone in a waiting room, six hours straight, sleepless, certain of her death, staring at a white double door that never opened.

But now, his focus is not on Monique. It's on José.

"Donor or recipient?" Hamilton says, raising his hand and looking straight into José's eyes, his voice surprisingly clear.

"What?" the man frowns, his gun pointed at Alex's head.

Hamilton nods with his chin to José's belly. "The chevron incision, right? You donated or received a liver. Like my wife." Liver transplant incisions often created a recognizable pattern like the one on Monique's torso, one which would always be there as a reminder of the Day. José probably had a Day as well. Everyone has at least one.

"Donor," José mumbles, tightening his jaw. *That man is a lot more Alex than Fraj0linha.*

"And you get that condo healthcare?" Hamilton says, more at ease than ever before. It's like he's talking with a friend. Beside him, Alex and the other co-op volunteers stare at him with gritted teeth and their suspicious eyes. "He pays you well, that I know, but do you get the same healthcare as him? Because there was a time when money could buy health but not anymore. Now you need people like us. You probably know that, judging by your scars."

"You want to die first, man?" José says, voice wavering.

"I want you to understand what you're killing. Not just us, nurses and lettuce pullers. An entire hospital. It is up to you if you think what Fraj0linha does with this boat is worthier than what we would do."

A daughter, a husband, a wife, a mother, a friend, an unknown person. There are people in our lives we'd gladly give parts of ourselves because without these people we wouldn't be entire. During those long seconds that stretch infinitely as the yacht sways on the rolling waters where Rio marries the ocean, Hamilton is sure he's going to die. He looks one last time at Monique, and all he has to offer is his smile. One that conveys apology as well as gratitude.

José pulls something from his pocket. Hamilton flinches.

"Let them go," José says, extending the pillbox to Hamilton. The others look suspiciously at him, but it's clear whom they respect. They all lower their weapons. "And leave the yacht with them."

8. Lying to your loved one about the (new) yacht in the harbor

"Another one?" Monique gapes at the new yacht in the co-op harbor. It's smaller than the Saúdiate—okay, Monique actually hates the name, so a change is pending—with a hull painted in indigo blue. She rubs her brow. "Our yacht is already operating. What did you do now, Hamilton?"

Hamilton stares at her, straight-faced. He grabs and squeezes her hands. With his other hand, he pats the new yacht. "We'll need more, so I stole another one, my love."

She laughs out loud and elbows him. "I know you're lying."

Hamilton pulls her closer. Alex hops aboard the new yacht. This one is for Trepadeira, and Hamilton is almost sure Alex will want to call it The Lettuce Sailor. According to him, it's the ideal name for a boat that will transport food to the most affected regions of Rio. Despite their inability to properly baptize boats, Hamilton's eyes moisten when he thinks about how many families their co-op can help now. Food and health are the bases of all societies, but they were taken from Rio even before the Atlantic invaded. If they can help reestablish those bases, even if slowly and sparsely, then all they're doing is already worth it.

"Bioreactors coming in!" Alex shouts from a watchtower at the harbor's entrance as a catamaran slows down. The community cops have been lending a few hands, helping them enlarge their security infrastructure. "Dock seven!

And the Saúdiate will be coming next. Two successful surgeries today! Plus three new kidneys have grown in the boat's lab. That's a win, right, folks?" People at the harbor clap and hoot. "And always keep our eyes trained on any minions from the influencer. But guess he's short-staffed now."

"Who's piloting that catamaran?" Monique squints at the man in the cockpit, who waves to Alex. "Is that—"

It was a sister, Hamilton discovered weeks later. José donated 60% of his liver to her. It gave her three more years. If not for the lack of resources in José's community, his sister could've lived longer.

"Guess sometimes we're lucky," Hamilton says, shrugging at Monique, while José and the former influencer's security team enter the harbor.

A SHORELINE OF OIL AND INFINITY

This is a story that snakes through sadness and hope, and one very dear to me because it shows that hope is not something that needs a specific state of mind. It can exist whether you're happy, sad, or think there's no way out. It's what attaches us to life at all times. The end of hope is the end of self. It's also a ghost town story, except the ghost is comprised of the fauna, flora, and the citizens (specially the children) of Saquarema. And the one responsible for the ghost's murder is the massive oil spillage on the beaches.

This is the snippet I published with the story in its original publication at Escape Pod:

"This story is set in Saquarema, a town in Rio de Janeiro state weaved between a lagoon and the Atlantic. All places mentioned in the story, with the exception of the supertanker, are real.

The Saquarema Lagoon biodiversity is enormous and it's home to a lot of different species of fish. The story imagines a tragic (but sadly possible) future where the town has suffered from a major oil spillage, but healing is still a possibility for the future. The tatuí (Emerita brasiliensis) is a tiny crustacean who drills holes in sandy beaches. Its presence often indicates the environmental quality of a beach, since it disappears from polluted areas."

. . . . **.** . **.** . . .

Conchinha
Charging... 87%
Energy source: light
Message:
Good morning, Vitória. The water is cold today. Brrr.

Vitória switches off the feed from her lenses and pats the tatuí's shell, kneeling before it.

"Hey, Conchinha." She brushes off the excess of crusted oil from the bot, scanning her fingerprint to open its main compartment. A wave breaks on the shore, sprinkling on her face and the bot. "Let's see what you have here."

The tatuí whirs—almost purrs. She plucks out the cylindrical cell from its rounded back. More darkened water. She doesn't read the full report, but she can guess what it contains pretty well. Heavy metals, volatile organic compounds, hydrocarbons... All there is to know in Barra Nova's waters these days. Layers of oil expand across both sides of the straight shoreline, coating the once-gilded sand, patches of darkness suffusing the air with the stink of hydrogen sulfide that in the past made the kids call that beach The Coast of Broken Eggs. André's kids—Vitória always thinks of them as her stepbrother's children, though not one of them was his by birth.

Vitória tucks the tatuí's cell, and the biome packs into her backpack and passes it over her shoulders.

"Thank you, little one. Add that sample's report to what we have and update our graphs." She taps the tatuí's shell, and it beeps, a strip of light gleaming blue along its surface. She sprays a water-sorbent-dispersant solution over it and wipes away the oil smudges from the bot as best as she can. Not enough. Never is. Oil impregnates everything, from the sand to the waters, from her tatuís to her grimy fingernails and her greasy curly hair. At home, it isn't rare to find small patches besmirching the parquet flooring, breadcrumbs leading her back to the beach, back to her work. And if she could look, there would probably be oil within her soul, too.

She lifts Conchinha to her thigh. It uses its suctioning legs to glue easily to her mycosynth suit's fabric. She blinks and opens a channel with the Tatuí Central Server, an incredibly unsophisticated computer chassis open at her desk, right next to her window for better ventilation. Her eyes flitting, she selects seven of the tatuís and resumes her walk across the beach, feet sticking to the oil, parting the rhythmic canticle of waves.

Barra Nova was never crowded. Even before the Spill, the coast was a temple for peace, a defiantly silent shoreline against the violent backdrop of the waves that pulled in and out, receding with intensity as if wanting to feed on the beach's serenity. Now, it's more than empty. It's deadened. She's the only one as far as the eye can see. Across the road up the beach on her left, houses line up, mostly left behind by families who couldn't withstand the staining of their horizon. On her right, *Petrocargo*. The 500-meter supertanker had been wrecked for five years, a looming ruin obtruding from the water, memory of a deceased way of life with its exposed pipes and its corroded, reddened deck slightly bent toward the beach.

"Oi, little friends!" she says to the tatuís she summoned. They assemble around her, skittering across the sand. Three stick to her legs and the smaller ones infiltrate her pockets—she doesn't even see them arriving but knows they're there because her lenses flash with brief yellow icons. "We have more healing for today—and destruction for some of you." She grins to herself. There are over 2,000 tatuís spread along Barra Nova Beach, *Petrocargo*, and the enormous Saquarema Lagoon at the other side of the few blocks that cut the shore. All tatuís have multiple directives. They could analyze the damaged environment to bring her data to act upon; they could pick up trash in an almost old-fashioned way, sucking it into their compartments; or they could bioremediate the shoreline, spreading the adequate mixtures and trying to maintain ideal conditions for its recovery.

A tatuí pings her lenses with an interrogation mark. It comes from the water. She turns and crouches. It's Joaninha. Some of the tatuís she recognizes at a distance. Joaninha is one of them. A giant version, at least in appearance, of the ladybugs she used to let scamper across her fingers in her home's backyard while André separated the fishes of the day into different baskets, whistling songs she could never recognize. She even painted Joaninha's shell with black spots, only to realize later that the oil blotted it with cruder, fuzzier blemishes.

"I love all of you," she says. "But I have to confess you all stink pra caramba." Not rotten eggs for her, but gas stations. And not the kind you stop by to eat snacks and catch a beer on road trips with your stepbrother.

Vitória loads up Joaninha's feed when it approaches.

> *Joaninha*
> *Charging... 47%*
> *Energy Source: light*
> *Oleophilic Fertilizers: 66%*
> *Microbial Remediation Compounds: 26%*
> *Phytoremediation Compounds: 42%*
> *Message:*
> *Oi, Vitória. I've found a fishing lure.*

Vitória bites her lips and clumsily presses her fingerprint to unlock the compartment and remove the cell. Her heart acts funny. She fidgets with the lid and lets the contents drop into her hand, a blend of sticky oiled water, sand, and... a small, tarnished swordfish with widened eyes. One of André's lures.

Vitória had only ever fished under her stepbrother's watch and never considered she knew anything besides how to clumsily spool a reel. What she really liked about it was to sway in the *Rainha Janaína*—André's motorized boat—with perhaps five or six children from Saquarema, the scent of coffee and salt and fish hanging like spray in the air while André told stories in his lilting, mesmerizing voice. Of raging storms, of gleaming fishes sparkling like lightning underwater, of the languages of the tide, of the motherly realms of Iemanjá.

André always fished on Saquarema Lagoon, and it was easier to find him there than at home. Though they lived together, he often slept in a rented shack by the lagoon's coastline—and sometimes on the *Rainha Janaína,* with 'the *nightly bafejo kissing your cheeks,*' as he put it. The sea was Iemanjá's body, he used to say, so that was not his realm to disturb. The lagoon, on the other hand, was Iemanjá's soul, a gift to the people of Saquarema, its salty body of water separated from the shoreline by a cluster of streets and houses less than a kilometer wide. At times, he removed his necklace—a small green lure depicting a silverside—and closed his eyes at the bow of the Rainha Janaína, mouthing words of security and peace to the mother of all orixás.

Other times, he sat on the gunwale and asked questions of the kids, hanging shiny, colorful fishing lures on his long black beard. Whenever one of them got a correct answer, he'd let them pick a prize.

What's the first thing to do after catching a fish?

What are lines, hooks, rods, reels, baits, lures, gaffs, and nets?

How do you fish under the gaze of Iemanjá?

And, most importantly, not a question at all but an aphorism—almost a request he always said at the end, delivering the kids back to the pier: *We have to occupy the evil places and make them good.*

It felt natural that André vanished from the city—and from her life—about the same time the kids did.

Vitória washes the fishing lure in a shower people once maintained near the sidewalk—and that she maintains by herself now, channeling clean water from the few treatment sites managed by the city hall. There's nothing indicating that the golden swordfish with a broken hook belonged to André. But there hadn't been anything that told her he would disappear three years after the Spill, yet she woke up that day feeling a weight in the air, knowing a storm was coming. Sitting up on her bed a few minutes before sunrise, she'd known that André didn't sleep in his shack by the Lagoon.

Like she *knows* the lure is one of his.

She holds it up under the sunlight. Probably a prize he gave to a kid after a correct answer. Something later abandoned as the kid moved from Saquarema and forgot about the black-bearded moço da Lagoa, the Lure Magician, the Barbudo of the Waters that silently walked around the city center buying groceries and fishing equipment, but who never held back from teaching them new stuff.

"Joaninha, where did you find this?" She holds it in front of the tatuí's scanner, a mere black dot at the front of its shell. But she only asks because she likes exact answers.

Joaninha
Charging... 49%
Energy Source: light
Message:
At the place I don't like :-(

The coordinates follow. Vitória raises her head and stares at the horizon she'd like to get rid of. She tries. Day and night, unceasingly, some of her tatuís are equipped with biomethylation modules to help corrode *Petrocargo*. But deep down, she knows it will never happen. No company, no government will ever come to remove the supertanker from her beach—from Iemanjá's body—and during her lifetime, no amount of tatuís will ever be able to make that wrecked temple of evil vanish like what happened to the real tatuís, the mullets, the bicudas... the kids...

The nightmares are the worst. They often come when she spends too much time thinking of Petrocargo during the day. She can scrub oil stains from her parquet flooring, but she can't ever wash away the blackened blood that slicks out of her arteries when she's dreaming. She's often in the Municipal Cemetery during those dreams, and Nossa Senhora de Nazaré Church, which is right next to the cemetery, doesn't exist. Multiple slits spontaneously open up along her arms, dripping oil into an empty grave, overflowing it with blackness. She always wakes up when she tries to read the name on the tombstone. She knows there's a name written on it, but she can't ever read it.

Iemanjá has left this city, Vitória told André days after the Spill. He nodded at her remark as if knowing it already. Perhaps he did. In those days, he rarely said anything. Perhaps for him Iemanjá had abandoned them a few years before the Spill when the oil tankers started cruising Barra Nova from side to side after the discovery of a pre-salt layer. Or, perhaps, Iemanjá could never leave them at all because she wasn't in the city, but she was the city. All those questions wandered through her mind at the time, but she never did ask him.

The kids that had once flocked around André's stories slowly dispersed after the Spill, scattered by the chaos that ensued. But before, many of them would use canoes to reach the new ruin that sprouted near the shore. Vitória shouted at them, urging them to come back, telling them of the dangers.

But it became their new adventure. And when she realized she'd do the same if she were a kid, she stopped shouting. Kids were curious. For them, it was like visiting an abandoned church in the countryside or venturing into mysterious woodlands. Instead of uselessly scowling at them, Vitória would find unspoiled patches of sand to sit on and hear the gurgling of the waves, uselessly trying to wash away the oil by closing her eyes.

The wind plucks at her dress. The scent of candle wax leaks out from Nossa Senhora de Nazaré Church behind her, the indistinct canticle of a mass seeping through the salt and oil across the air. She flicks the golden swordfish between her fingers, sitting on a stone and overlooking the Municipal Cemetery, Saquarema Bridge, and the Lagoon beyond it.

The trees ruffle around the cemetery, and mournful seagulls fly above the church, crooning for their spoiled habitat. She tucks the fishing lure into her pocket and walks to the undertaker's tiny cabin. She knocks lightly on the door. He's a humped man with furry eyebrows and the smile of someone who knows all the secrets beyond the grave. He pats the tatuí she gave him two years before—which he plastered full of stickers.

The man's eyes shine in silver for a second, and she recalls how he and André helped her test her prototype tatuís years before. Both sat on the beach with their eyes gleaming with the tatuís' feeds, the still rough cube-shaped bots bustling about their legs and feet.

The man shakes his head. Negative. Not yet. Maybe never. His smile slightly wavers—and hers, soon after.

Vitória rarely visits the ruin. She doesn't fear the dark, endless corridors, slightly crooked, and the abandoned accommodations, empty and eaten up by moss. She has grown used to the stink as if every molecule in the air itself had been smudged with petroleum and rust and mildew. What she doesn't like is the ruin's lament, the way it sings unevenly, tuneless, the walls creaking and clanking and clattering, hidden pipes blowing whatever breath they still have within them. Even her tatuís' A.I. systems, a biased reflection of her mind, have decided they don't like *Petrocargo*.

Foquinha has brought her here, a canoe-sized tatuí, one of her largest, which she uses only when navigating somewhere. She has brought Joaninha and a few smaller ones attached to her mycosynth suit, and now they skitter along a darkened corridor, casting their lights on the path and showing her the way to where Joaninha found the fishing lure.

We have to occupy the evil places and make them good. It's harder to think on those terms inside the supertanker. She's at the root of all evil. Vitória grimaces when her feet shiver on the uneven floor. The tanker groans, reading her thoughts.

"Joaninha," she whispers. "Are we there yet?"

Joaninha and the other tatuís turn right and stop at a dead end. Joaninha casts a blue halo across the floor. The place where it found the lure.

Vitória pats the LED on Joaninha's shell so it knows it can dim the light and save its battery.

There's nothing else there, but at the end of the corridor, she sees an entrance covered with a muslin curtain fluttering with the stale wind that finds its way through the tanker's recesses. Someone has drawn a smiley face on the fabric.

She loads the tatuís on her lenses and asks them to go inside with their lights on. She shivers a little. Not because she doesn't know what she's going to find but because she does. Her tatuís had already informed her of those things.

They're in many places around the ship. Mostly toys the kids left scattered in their adventures. They must have kept them at the tanker knowing they'd come back soon, knowing they could make a base to explore the place and forget their parents talking about the economic recession gnawing at city and country, about the death of animals and plants, about leaving everything behind...

Vitória paces slowly around the small room, careful not to kick the stuff left behind, Joaninha guiding her steps. A storeroom, probably used for cleaning items when the tanker was still operating. Now, those forgotten items are replaced by dice, board games, wireless toy trucks, ship models, plush fishes, shrimps, sushi, and even books, neatly organized and undisturbed on a metal shelf by the corner. At the far side of the storeroom lies a broken wooden board with a single item atop it. A toppled Iemanjá statuette made of resin, her blue dress, long black hair, and brown skin pockmarked by moss, but mostly preserved. Vitória smiles alone in the dark and turns the idol up.

"Joaninha, relay a message to the others for me. I want you to make a catalog of everything around here and bring the small stuff back home."

The last time she saw André, they were aboard the *Rainha Janaína*. He'd taken them to the middle of the lagoon, to the most equidistant part from all the shores, as if he wanted to escape the city by infinitely converging into the water. André had a dead carapicú on his lap with glazed, unfocused eyes and greenish spots smudging its scales. So far into the lagoon, the wind didn't reek of oil, but a mustiness clung to the air. Three years had passed since the Spill, and the water had shifted its colors from verdigris to a nauseating lime. Algae bloom was one of the uncountable consequences. Many species had disappeared by then, and it was a matter of time until the struggling survivors found their demise.

Saquarema was a lot emptier from a massive exodus, too. Restaurants had closed their business, tourism had dwindled, and the beaches became coastal deserts. Even the kids risking themselves sneaking into *Petrocargo* had moved away with their families, their friendships disbanded, their adventures a memory.

André had always been a silent man, except when telling stories to the kids. That day, he said only one thing.

How can you occupy an evil place that big, maninha?

He didn't take his eyes off the dead fish on his lap. Vitória remained silent then, but later, reminiscing about that day, she realized André really wanted to know her answer, if she had one. She didn't, anyway.

They stood quiet for many minutes, the wind spraying salt on their faces. André always liked quiet moments, most of all during those last days. All Vitória wanted was to sway lightly with the boat, to stay there with her stepbrother, as quiet as they used to be when their mother died—she was sixteen years old then—and they sat mute on the backyard grass to avoid waking up their father's ire for whatever reason.

André had saved her life once. Their father wanted them to work on the docks like him. For him, it was the only work his children could ever do because he had *bred such whiny weaklings*. Whenever his Fiat Uno roared into the garage, Vitória was prepared to leap across the backyard wall and disappear with a duffel bag into the streets leading to the lagoon. Sometimes she'd spent hours away from home. And when she dared, she'd sleep at a friend's or even—as she did twice—walk eight kilometers along the beach, hoping it would stretch and become infinite. She couldn't stand her father's lessons, which often involved going with him to the docks and carrying heavy boxes from place to place in what seemed to be purposeless rearrangements. And every time she fled, it was with the knowledge that later she'd have to hear screams and sometimes a glass or a plate breaking. But as long as André stood grave like a totem by her side, her father wouldn't touch any of them. And André seemed to know exactly when to be there.

When she started enrolling in online automation classes, André watched in silence behind her, sometimes whistling lowly, a sound that calmed her. And when she started assembling shelled bots for her projects, she glimpsed the smile underneath his shaggy beard. She told him she wanted to live in Rio de Janeiro for a while, just to graduate in control and automation engineering, so he stole his father's Uno and drove her and her bulky luggage there. He was twenty-three at the time, four years older than herself. She knew he spent months—perhaps years—listening to sermons and hearing how despicable a son he was for dumping his *fragile irmãz-inha in a giant city*. When she came back five years later, her father had already vanished with his Uno. She thought of asking André if he did something, anything that could've scared him away.

But she didn't. Silence had always been their friend.

When André vanished, he left only a brief note on a torn piece of paper stuck to a tatuí on her table.

I need it more than anything. Goodbye, maninha. Te amo.

Apart from peeking at the obituaries in the first weeks after his vanishing, Vitória refrained from looking him up or trying to find out what he did with his life. In his eyes, he had already departed when *Petrocargo* sailed the waters of Saquarema.

The blue of her dress is different; the brown of her skin and the black of her hair are sharper. Even the gilded colors of her seashell-crusted crown gradually change while the smallest tatuís scoot throughout the statuette, cleaning it, and removing five-year-old moss and mildew. Beside it on the workbench, other tatuís take care of a couple of books and the ship model Vitória brought from *Petrocargo*.

She'd like to go after the owners of those items, perhaps see the smiles of finding things thought long lost.

Vitória's lenses flash with a proximity alert from her central server. She blinks twice and moves her eyes to the left to open a connection.

A list of names and locations appears: Areia, 24 meters; Azulão, 25 meters; Estrela da Rainha, 26 meters... Many of her medium and big-sized tatuís coming back? She hears a loud whir outside and hurries to the front gate. Hundreds of them cross the street from the beach. She reopens a connection and skims through their reports, trying to find a pattern.

Pictures of statuettes and, in some cases, the objects themselves appear on her lenses. Iemanjá, Saint George, Oxossi, Saint Sebastian, Jesus, Ogum, Xangô...

Vitória crouches and picks up a small Saint George's idol from Azulão's compartment, the dragon underneath defiled by moss. On the bottom, written in blue crayon: *The Lure Magician said we should shun the gods of oil by bringing ours.*

A tear crosses her cheeks. That storeroom—and all the others hidden in the darkness of the tanker—filled with toys isn't only an abandoned base for child's play. It is that and so much more. It's a temple erected by the kids. A place of evil occupied by good.

A ping pops up in her lenses, incessantly seeking her attention. A tatuí jostles the others and plops open its compartment, releasing a tiny, still glossy, green silverside.

She doesn't always dream of graves and oil. Sometimes, she's not in the cemetery at all but stepping barefoot on white sand gilded by the sun. In those dreams, Vitória always looks ahead and knows the shoreline stretches infinitely.

The breeze wafts the aroma of wet earth and the flowers the undertaker's pruning toward her, completely overcoming the oil-ridden air. Around the Nossa Senhora de Nazaré's tower, seagulls sing their songs, and a fog hovers in Barra Nova Beach, completely cloaking *Petrocargo*.

When André vanished, Vitória knew he had a friend who would never stop looking for him, one who knew where people settled when there was nowhere else to go. And even though she respected André's last wish, she fed herself throughout the years with the same hope she nurtures about seeing her beach, her lagoon, and her city healed—a queasy tightness in her chest, a stubbornness that insists life always finds ways to impregnate what's dead.

She touches the undertaker's elbow. His tatuí emits a subtle hum, making circling patterns over a small bromeliad field. He turns toward her, smiling, and points to the tatuí.

Vitória loads its feed on her lenses, but the answer is already on the smiling eyes of a friend.

Ikú
Charging... 77%
Energy source: light

Message:
Olá! There's someone in the lagoon.

Vitória hasn't seen a real tatuí since a few months after the Spill—the *Emerita brasiliensis*, that minute, grey-shelled crustacean that lent their name to her bots, is one of the many species that disappeared. The only things her tatuís bring back to her from those creatures are their tiny, hardened, oil-clad shells.

But now there's one gamboling at her feet on the Saquarema Lagoon shore. She crouches, picks it up, and lets it scurry along her palm like she did when she was a kid on the beach, waiting for them to caper out of her hand and drill their tiny holes into the sand to disappear. It circles the lures on her palm, finding a path along her index finger.

When she turns her hand to keep looking at it, the creature leaps off and quickly vanishes into a hole it bores for itself.

She sits on the pier's edge, her feet slightly touching the water. She stares at the silhouette of a fisherman floating on the lagoon and starts whistling a velvety song along with the wind.

SOIL OF OUR HOME, STORM OF OUR LIVES

This story was written in June 2020, when we still had little idea of the pandemic's real toil. Everything was already bleak, but also new, and people were starting to find meaning in their own homes. I'm not sure if that's why I decided to write about home and community. The real spark for this one came two years before, in 2018, when I read the news about an abandoned building collapsing in São Paulo. It had been occupied by homeless people encouraged by some social movements. Those movements were accused of putting people in danger, but all they were doing was finding a place for them to stay. If the state and the elite don't really care about them, we can't blame those who do, even if their actions are harsh. That's what made me think of the Wrecking Balls, perceived as terrorists by the public, but actually just trying to make a difference to a group of climate refugees.

This is also a story about family and finding yourself in (and out) of it. One of the cores of Soil of Our Home, Storm of Our Lives is its "skeleton," which is made up of past, present, and future. The past (Alzira meeting the Wrecking Balls and starting to change the face of her town) means revolution and change; the present (Jota telling the town's story to his daughter) means consolidation and education. And the future (Célia's wonder about her town, her world, and her grandmother) is what's hidden in the story, but perhaps the most important part of it: turning into commonplace what was outrageous and absurd years before. When Célia comes of age, perhaps a group like the Wrecking Balls will never be seen as terrorists by anyone.

· · · · ● · ● · · ·

It was only a matter of time until he saw the bruises on his daughter's face.

Célia's left eye was blackened and her lips were blotched with blood. Dollops of mud ran down from her cheeks to her upper lip. Her hands were clasped in front of her, smeared with sludge and shame. Her eyes had welled up, but she wasn't crying. Her grandma, Alzira, used to say one must have a pretty good reason to cry, and Jota knew Célia couldn't decide what exactly was a good reason. He couldn't either.

"*Amor*, tell me what happened." Jota crouched before her, gently clutching her right hand and settling the ice bag on it. He recognized the stain of blood smeared on her swollen lips, the tiny droplets dabbing her chin. He knew damn well the mud came from the olericulture compound next to Aramá's Elementary School, where the students had complementary activities. And if things hadn't changed so much, that mud tasted a bit like radish.

"This boy called Grandma a terrorist." Célia wept, probably deciding that was a good reason to cry. In his time, he often thought it was too until he learned to ignore the provocations directed at him or his mother.

Célia raised the ice bag and put it underneath her left eye. Jota rubbed the mud from her face and hands with a towel, then pulled her into a hug, smiling so she would know everything was fine.

"He said..." Célia wept close to his ear. "He said she was an... ugly demolition ball and a terrorist."

Jota sighed, standing.

"Let's go for a walk, *amor*." Jota pulled Célia onto the sidewalk. "Breathe slowly... On your pace." His mother did the same the first time an older boy punched him and said he was the son of landless filth.

Sunlight reflected along the windmills' blades of Aramá's wind factories. There were more people than usual on the streets. The city's biggest June Party would start later and visitors arrived from Parapeúna, Valença, and even farther from Rio de Janeiro and Belo Horizonte. At the end of the street, a woman repaired the biogas lampposts in front of Beckerfield. The sprouses lined up a soft slope from Beckerfield's fences, each house differing from the other in their treelike shapes. Between the sprouses, photovoltaic poles were bedecked with the party's colored flags.

"Let's rest here." Jota turned below one of the purifier tanks that recycled water from the vast storm drains surrounding Aramá. "There are things about Grandma you need to learn."

"Is it true she protected... terrorists? That she..."

"That she was a terrorist herself? Of course not, sweetie. People who call her that don't really know her." They were becoming fewer each year, but Aramá had its share of people who didn't know the city's history. Often the wrong assumptions came from the children of Rio de Janeiro landowners enrolled in Aramá's schools because they'd become famous as the country's best.

Jota grabbed Célia's backpack and sat on a bench. She sat beside him, wiping tears and the remaining mud off her face.

Once, his mother had told him the city hadn't always smelled like this. But that was so part of it—of him—that it was hard to notice unless he focused and sniffed the air. The sylvan scent that the breeze shoved from the sprouses was also how he remembered his mother, stooped over a tablet, programming what one day would be their future.

"What was she, then, Dad?" Célia asked.

"She never found out. Sometimes she introduced herself as a gardener, other times as a programmer. Not so commonly, a rebel."

The bastards...

Alzira closed the kitchen shutters, as instructed by the prefecture, and turned back to the stockpot where she was cooking baião de dois—rice, green beans, coalho cheese—to feed the displaced people established near the golf course.

If it wasn't enough that her town was becoming a hub for Rio de Janeiro's evacuees, now terrorists were passing through.

Let the storm pass, Mami used to say. It was a good strategy. Just wait. Most things did pass if you let them go.

Her phone's screen flashed on the counter. She stooped to look at it. Not Marcos. Just a local news update notification. Of course, it wasn't the man for whom she promised a life, then abandoned overnight one year ago because she was on the verge of breaking out...

"... and the Wrecking Balls are driving through RJ-147 toward Rio Preto," said a grave voice in her mobile. *"The terrorist group will be passing through Aramá at any moment. The police are still giving chase. Stay at home. If you see anything suspicious, use your public security app to send your location to the police."*

She scraped her teeth, turned off the news report, and resumed dropping chopped onion into the stockpot. *Just ignore...*

The Wrecking Balls. Brazil's budding terrorist group passing through her town. Great... She didn't know much about them, though. They assassinated landowners, blew up properties, and destroyed construction sites in the countryside.

An engine roared in the quiet street outside. Brakes pulled. Too close.

Just avoid it... Not all storms have to be contained by you.

The living room door burst open.

"But how was she a gardener?" Célia frowned, putting down the ice bag and wiping the remaining mud stains off her face with purified water Jota had given her. "I never saw Grandma planting anything."

"When you were born, she'd already stopped." Jota straightened the disheveled tufts of Célia's hair and tied them with her hairpin. A prolonged beep sounded across the city, reminding everyone that the thermal energy towers were switching on for the night.

"You said the cops had orders to... kill?" Célia pointed at a cop duo pedaling across the field, leisurely heading toward Beckerfield. "They seem nice, though."

He'd always been reticent to tackle sensible matters with Célia. But she was nine years old and just had her face smacked. Jota was ten when his mother had placed him on the kitchen counter and told him what she did and why he had to be exceedingly careful on the streets. Luckily, things were safer for Célia.

"The cops are not the same," Jota said. "They were... a different kind of police back then... The Order Squad."

Célia gaped at him and put a finger over her mouth, thinking.

"And the displaced people you mentioned? Are they gone, right? The teacher says we're gonna talk about displacement and refuge next month."

Jota waved at the cops.

"Well..." He shrugged. "There are no more displaced people in Aramá. But they're not gone at all."

There were two terrorists inside her house. Inside Mami's house. They were named Alfredo and Gui as they didn't seem to be worried about hiding their names while talking with each other. The only thing they'd asked of her was a first aid kit, so she grabbed the one Marcos had given her as a gift and that she'd never used.

Alfredo was a black man wearing a dark turtleneck and

frayed jeans. He was a few years older than Alzira: bald, face stubbled with an unshaven beard, sporting a necklace with an almond-shaped pendant. His leg was hurt, and he'd come in toppling, falling to the sofa and groaning, more from disappointment than from pain.

Gui was a blonde young man in his twenties, acne scars mottling his cheeks. He wore a waist bag and his t-shirt stated *"If you move fast and break things, you might break yourself."* Upon entering, he'd dumped an ecobag next to her TV rack.

Now Alzira stood in the middle of the living room with her hands clasped on her legs, eyes panning back and forth over them. They didn't carry guns, not anything visible, at least.

Gui kneeled and grimaced at the blood on his partner's jeans.

"Sorry for breaking in," Alfredo said, face twitching in pain.

She nodded because that was the only thing left to do. But was it still her house? The Wrecking Balls were famous for taking possession of properties, and their invasion might mean they'd just gotten one more. It'd been here where she'd learned how to cook, Mami's steady hand steering hers, blending tapioca flour with shrimp to make tacacá. It was at the rustic wooden table opposite the door that she'd learned to code on an outdated computer, dreams of big cities force-fed by virtual, unreachable colleagues.

"Be still, Alfredo." Gui pushed Alfredo back into the sofa and clicked the health kit open.

"I'm just tired." Alfredo wheezed, pulling up his jeans. The wound was above his right ankle and was spattered with blood. "Only a graze caused by the drone shot."

"We may have to run." Gui glowered at him. "And you

can't run like this." He inspected the first aid kit, fingers hovering over plasters, sterile gauze dressings, bandages, tweezers, and... back to plasters. He had no idea what he was doing.

"May I?" Alzira said.

Gui inspected her, frowning, then stepped aside.

Alzira kneeled before Alfredo. Taking care of a terrorist in her own house wasn't what she'd had in mind when she exchanged Rio for Aramá. But the quicker she dealt with the duo, the quicker they'd leave her alone.

"What's your name?" Alfredo said.

"Alzira." Alfredo's blood oozed close to where Mami sat to watch soap operas. Alzira gently pulled his leg aside so it wouldn't stain the fake leather.

"I like names that start with 'Al'." He grinned. "Reminds me everything will be alright."

Gui scoffed. "Can't believe you're losing your leg and still making stupid jokes." He was peeking through the shutters. Alzira saw their dark green car properly parked on the sidewalk. Not smashing the flowers she'd cultivated when she arrived in an attempt to make the house look more like something Mami would love and less like the place she'd left unattended after Mami died.

"I'm not losing anything, boy." Alfredo grunted when Alzira touched his wound with a sterile dressing. "Hey, hey, easy!"

"You told him you're fine, man," Alzira said, spraying more antiseptic into the wound. He bit his shirt's sleeve. "So behave as if it's true."

Alfredo's groan switched to laughter. His wound wasn't serious. But it needed cleaning and bandaging to avoid infection.

All she knew about first aid she'd learned from Marcos.

She was twenty-two when she exchanged Mami and Aramá's peace for the chaos of a dying Rio. Marcos was twenty-five, a medical student, a glint in his eyes when he looked at her, mouth full of promises about the future, *their* future. Mami had told her Rio was no place for peace and prospects. *The future begins right here*, she used to say, though Alzira never quite figured out what she meant by that. Aramá was a far smaller city a decade ago, three or four dozen isolated houses spread around the golf course where the wealthy folks from Rio went to play. In the big city, the sea was creating an economic and humanitarian crisis across the streets, drowning homes, forcing tiny houses to bundle up three... six... nine more people than they should. Yet, Alzira always thought of herself as a woman who marched against the tide. Today she knew: she needed the thrill back then, the uncertainty of chasing storms and becoming someone besides the young countryside girl who earned a computing degree from an online college. So she went, dreams and risks stuffed in her backpack.

"You're good to go," Alzira said, rolling down Alfredo's pants leg.

"Thank you," Alfredo said. "Actually, I feel like nothing has happened. Are you a doctor?"

"Unemployed computer scientist."

"Who does the work of a doctor. I told you we were lucky," Alfredo said to Gui, standing and stumbling toward the table. Gui pulled out a chair for him.

Alzira felt a knot in her stomach. They were all at the table now. Like her, Uncle Thiago, and Aunt Kelly had been years ago, drinking beer and talking loud, waiting for Mami's tacacá. Only these people were strangers. One of the things she feared when she broke up with Marcos and moved back to Aramá was finding that her hometown wasn't part of her anymore. That without her mother—the house's soul—there wouldn't be anything for her there, and she could simply not find the peace of mind she was looking for. And staring up at these two, smudging her table with hands dirtied with soil, she realized her fears might be creeping in faster than she thought.

"Hey, lady," Gui said.

"Her name is Alzira," Alfredo said. At first, she thought he was mocking her, but his face was serious.

"Alzira," Gui said, rolling his eyes. He removed a paper-thin tablet from his waist bag and tapped on it. "How long does it take to get to the golf course?"

"Beckerfield? About ten minutes." She packed the first aid tools back inside the kit, looking sideways at the ecobag they'd dropped on the floor. Inside were several brown spheres flaked with dirt. Her gut lurched. Bombs? Inside Mami's house?

"Come sit with us," said Alfredo. "We might stay here for a while. Our car broke."

"Broke is not technically right," Gui said, still focused on his tablet. "We're out of charge."

"I told you." Alfredo's eyes gleamed in genuine worry. "We're bad planners."

"We lack resources."

"Bad planners often run out of resources." Alfredo lowered his head on his hands.

Alzira sat at the other side of the table, facing the door behind the duo. They stank of an excessively traveled dirt road moldering under a weeklong rain.

An uncharged car, the two of them sitting with their backs to the door, no care to hide their identities... Yep, bad planners. But they didn't seem the kind of people she'd call the police on, much less this new Order Squad that had been perpetrating atrocities across the state. Yet, they were terrorists. Invaders of Mami's house. If her mother was alive, she'd be after them with a broom and a repertoire of nasty words. No matter how disparate from her image of terrorists they were. They'd brought *bombs* inside her house.

She slipped her hands into her shorts' pocket and surreptitiously removed her phone, keeping it beneath the table. Her thumb hovered above the public security app. Just a touch. The cops would arrest those two and... *Kill them...*

Her hesitation was enough for Alfredo to raise his head and extend a hand to her with a sorry smile. She bit her lips and slid her phone across the table to him, unsure if she'd have touched the app.

"What's that smell?" Alfredo sniffed the air.

"Baião de dois," Alzira said, looking toward the kitchen to avoid his gaze. "I was cooking for the evacuees." The plates she'd picked for them were piled up on the counter, twenty in total, though the evacuee count was already over fifty and increasing daily.

"Baião de dois..." Alfredo opened a smile. "Aunt Alícia's favorite dish. She has a restaurant in Porto Velho. Been quite a few years since I've seen the woman..."

"Porto Velho in Rondônia?" Alzira's mouth hinted at a smile, but she forced a serious expression. "Mami was from there. She came to Rio as a child."

"See? It seems we have more than 'Al' in common." Alfredo looked down at his hands. His knuckles were stained black, his fingers callused with grime. "Aunt Alícia never had the money to visit me. I used to go there twice a year to see her, but now..."

Alfredo fidgeted with his necklace. The pendant had thin silver lines scrawled on its surface.

Alzira stood and walked to the kitchen. Mami used to say you shouldn't refuse food to a person. She'd cook for the neighborhood. *Delicious Northern Food. Help me pay my daughter's tuition.* But if there was someone who couldn't afford a dish, she'd give it freely. A few people certainly ripped her off, but Mami didn't care. *Food is not a possession*, she used to say.

When Alzira moved from Aramá to Rio seven years ago, she went with Mami's mind as her own. She volunteered on the beaches, helping to raise barriers that would impede the water from advancing. She lent her skills to relief units, programming apps that would help resettle the homeless and guide them out of the water's path. Her day jobs had all been with companies that promised to spring Rio out of bad times. But as the years passed, she realized she'd become a battered city heritage herself, like a building slowly eroded by the rising tide.

The duo didn't speak as she set the table with the pot of food and slid plates for them, serving generous portions of baião and filling two jars with water and ice.

"As my mother used to say, I have given you food, so now I have the upper hand. What's your business here?" She went back to her seat, surprised at the steadiness of her voice.

They exchanged looks.

"None of your business," Gui said, hesitant to take a spoonful of baião.

Alfredo scowled at him. "If you act like a damn terrorist, then that's what people will call us."

"You're terrorists," Alzira said. "I see the... explosives." She pointed with her chin to the ecobag beside the TV rack.

"The buds?" Alfredo snickered. "They're not bombs, Alzira." He raised a finger. "They might be dangerous, I give you that. Otherwise, the skull pigs wouldn't be chasing us. But they're not weapons. No one really chases criminals because of their weapons... Criminals are chased because of the risk they impose to some... castes of society."

"Why are you here, then?" She understood Mami now. Giving food to others at your own table, your own home, bestowed you with a kind of power and self-confidence.

"We're... houseculturists."

Gui giggled. "This name again? This is silly."

"Do you know every property has a social function, Alzira?" Alfredo ignored his partner, taking big mouthfuls of the baião. "This is delicious, by the way. Not like Aunt Alícia's, though, but... differently good. You put more cheese and I think it made it... I just—I love it. It makes me feel funny." He knocked his hands on the table and quirked up his mouth. "I wish I had the right word for it."

"Social function..." Alzira said, bringing the conversation back to the subject.

"All properties have a social function that's in our Constitution." Alfredo raised his fork, speaking with his mouth full. "It's wrong—not to say cruel—to keep idle lands in a moment like this when coastal cities are failing all along the country. What we do is ensure this part of our Constitution is fulfilled."

"Like the homeless and landless movements..." Alzira nodded, remembering how the Order Squad promised to chase social movements across the country. "You invade unused property and claim—"

Alfredo shook his head.

"We do something different..."

Gui glared at him.

"C'mon... If we want to refute the label of terrorists... If we don't want to be called the Wrecking Balls... We might as well start telling everyone *exactly* what we do."

Gui shook his head. Alfredo clamped his lips shut.

"So your business is in Beckerfield..." Alzira stooped to look at Gui's tablet. He pulled it back and glowered at her. He had a map centered on the golf course.

"It's been abandoned for a few years now," Alfredo said. "It's a sixty-hectare delusion. Did you ever see any Brazilian playing golf? It shouldn't have been built in the first place."

"How would you blow up a golf course? You might target the few corrupt companies exploiting the rivers nearby. If you set the course on fire, you're probably putting *my* city on fire, and I can't let you do that."

Speaking of Aramá in such a way made her chest tickle with something she hadn't felt since she established with Marcos in Rio and scrolled through a list of volunteer jobs, unaware the big city had a mouth large enough to crunch pieces of her.

"Who said anything about blowing up stuff, Alzira?" Alfredo said, his mouth full. "Forget bombs."

Gui stared up at him, scorn etching his face.

"Oh. All right. The government says we blow stuff up." Alfredo roared with laughter, then put a hand over his mouth when Gui slapped his shoulder.

Gui peeked out the window. It was growing dark. He eyed Alfredo, and they exchanged looks of mutual understanding.

"Alzira..." Alfredo snatched a napkin and wiped his mouth. "Can we stay for the night?"

"Why?" She asked more because she was becoming curious about their... mission. Oddly enough, their request to sleep in her house didn't strike as invasive to her. It felt like friends asking for a place to crash. Letting them spend the night should be wrong... Should *feel* wrong... Yet, it didn't. Something Mami said that compelled Alzira to help others when she arrived in Rio was that *you gotta treat everyone as good people until you see them do bad stuff*. And these two looked like brothers at the end of an exhaustive trip.

"Dark is dangerous," Alfredo said, standing and collecting his and Gui's plates and cutlery, then hobbling toward the kitchen. "We know the skull pigs' modus operandi. They remain undercover for twelve hours, no more than that, while their drones buzz around, seeking our faces. But they can't stay longer. There are other issues they'll have to deal with. Not enough skull pigs for too much crisis."

"Didn't they tag your car?"

Alfredo shook his head and grinned. "Gui's got gimmicks to fake GPS signals and a lovely device with nano-cells that changes the color of the vehicles we use. Pretty new tech."

Alfredo darted a look at Alzira from the kitchen, his grin fading into a taut jaw.

"Rest assured, we'll leave at morning's first light."

Alzira nodded, unable to verbally consent to their request but also unable to refuse. Unable to understand why, since before her plans in Rio started to crumble, she didn't feel empty. She should be disgusted with herself.

When the sun set and the street lampposts came on, Alfredo was doing the dishes and muttering a song under his breath.

"Does it hurt?" Jota cupped Célia's face, stopping on their way to Beckerfield. He inspected her eye. He knew it hurt.

In his time, it hurt a lot, though more in his heart. High school had been the worst. The city was in turmoil back then, and even national news was focusing on it. His mother had promised him it wouldn't last forever. He wouldn't have to worry about walking on the streets or meeting certain types of people at school. She'd put a lot of the blame on herself for being in the spotlight, but he knew she was doing what she could.

"It hurts," Célia said. "But it will get better."

He cast a smile at her. That mindset came from her grandma.

Up ahead, people were arriving for the first party night. They parked their electric bikes underneath the biogas lights. A crowd gathered in front of the Beckerfield's flag-decorated fences that years ago had been an imposing wall. Girls with braided hair wearing flowered dresses laughed with boys in straw hats, taking turns to write love letters that would be delivered by cyclists during the party.

A bonfire had been lit in front of the nearest sprouses. The breeze brought the scent of veggie dog and canjica. A stocky man—the city's police chief—was testing the microphones for the karaoke.

They entered Beckerfield. People waved at him and Célia from the sprouses' windows. The sprouses themselves had different shapes and sizes, giving the field different shades of personality. The Castro's sprouse looked like a bulky tree, while the Torres's resembled a wooden igloo. The Ferreiras were a big family, so they liked theirs cozily packed next to each other and shaped like balloons.

Célia nodded.

"I want to show you something." Jota clasped Célia's hand and pulled her amidst the sprouses.

"Will you tell me more of Grandma?" Célia said, glancing at all the games and small theaters lined up in nearby stalls. "And Grandpa, too. I remember he told me jokes."

"Yes, but first, I have a gift for you."

Célia whooped.

"What's it, Dad?" She tugged at his sleeve. "What?"

"It's a dollhouse."

The first light of the morning shone through the shutters before Alzira could sleep. She was lying on her mother's bed, staring up at the ceiling like she did when she decided to tell Marcos she wouldn't stay. He'd always supported her willingness to volunteer. But when she'd risen from bed that day, walked to the kitchen, and saw him there making cheese tapioca, he had the eyes of a man who knew he'd lost something. The next day, she left, disillusions stuffed in her backpack, but also maintaining a peace of mind that she hoped to cluster back together someday.

The light steps of someone came from the living room. She stood and quickly changed her clothes. Alfredo had slept on the sofa, supposedly guarding the door, and she'd given her bedroom to Gui.

Alfredo was peeking at the front door's broken lock. His were the eyes of a man with not much left to lose.

"Didn't want to wake you so early," he said. "I was going to try to fix this and then nudge that sleepyhead to get going. I didn't tell him, but I want this to be his last mission with me. He's behind in a lot of his classes."

Or maybe he still had a few things left to lose.

Alzira dismissed Alfredo with a gesture of his head. "Leave the lock."

"You have a backyard, right?" Alfredo said, straightening

his necklace.

She nodded. It was the place where Mami performed her experiments. Mami loved gardening but was never good at it. She could cultivate calendulas and candytufts in the front yard. Still, for each set of flowers glistening with dew in the pathway to the front door, Mami had a garden of failures in the back. Azaleas, ferns, orchids... When Alzira came from Rio for her mother's memorial, she'd found nothing in the backyard but a patch of watered, well-trimmed turf. No flowers. As if Mami had left that empty space so her only daughter could cultivate something.

"I want to show you something," Alfredo said. "Can we go outside?"

Alzira nodded.

She opened the backyard door in the kitchen. The grass was a bit overgrown, sneaking on the house's wall and the washing tank. She didn't have Mami's patience. Or Mami's love of yard work.

Alfredo peeked around the turf and decided on a spot right in the middle. He crouched before it and yanked the grass with his bare hands. She gaped at him, wanting to protest. Mami would smack his head with a broomstick. Instead, she lowered beside him when he gestured to her.

Alfredo removed his necklace and unfastened its almond-shaped pendant.

"This is our... bomb," he said, smiling, exuding that same earthy scent Gui also carried.

He tucked the pendant in the soil and covered it with earth, rubbing his hand to flatten the soil. He had a tablet folded on his belt. He removed and unfolded it like a parchment.

"Gui developed most of it," he said, tapping some icons.

"The guy is a genius."

The soil shifted. She blinked. Perhaps she was exhausted...

"This is a mini-version of our buds," Alfredo said. "Each bud contains millions of nano-meristems, bots designed to replicate a blueprint that's in this tablet. Almost any shape. It uses a mix of material from the soil and what we put in the bud itself. Gui knows the finer details, but it's mostly minerals, organic matter, gas, water..."

A flimsy brown shoot sprang up from the soil.

"It then follows a pre-defined algorithm that knows how to best use the available resources like a tree in a program. One of this size grows faster than a plant, but bigger ones take more time. By now, my pendant is torn apart."

After some minutes, the shoot swelled—first like a bubble, then forming vertices and acquiring a cubic shape. It was like watching a tree growing and rebelling against its usual growth patterns.

"Synthetic meristematic cells. What Gui calls merisynths increase the diameter of the house according to what's in the blueprint, preserving a heartwood in its middle, pretty much like a real tree. But instead of creating layer upon layer of wood inside it..." Holes appeared in the shape growing in her garden. One, two, three... A small door and two small windows. Alfredo squiggled his fingers inside. "... The blueprint defines how many empty spaces this tiny house... this sprouse... will have. Its rooms..."

The growth slowed. It looked like a miniature...

"Dollhouse..." Alfredo said. He slid a finger over its surface and knocked hard on it to show how resistant it was. "The bark protects it from the weather too. More importantly, we can program asbestos bark to grow and protect the houses from fire. It leaves the skull pigs disappointed." He flashed a grin at her.

"You're crying..." Alzira said. Tears streamed down Alfredo's cheeks. "You must have a very good reason to be crying."

"This was supposed to be a gift for Aunt Alícia." He caressed the dollhouse's angled rooftop.

"And why would you use it here?" She placed her hand over the hands of a man she had considered a terrorist a few hours before.

"We can do more." He wiped his tears. "But I've carried this one with me for a couple of years, and I always thought of Aunt Alícia when I looked at it. She was like a mother to me. I feared the authorities making connections, so I never returned to Porto Velho. Well..." He shrugged. "Sometimes life takes us into paths we don't expect."

He stood. Alzira helped him up when he grimaced, putting weight on his injured leg.

Alfredo looked at the tiny house once more. "That's what we do. That's our wrecking ball."

He walked back into the living room. Gui was already there, a reprimand etched on his face. Alfredo reached for his pocket and gave her mobile back to her with an apologetic face.

"People will remember this place, Alzira," he said.

The future begins right here.

Alzira had given herself too easily in the past. She'd gouged out bits of herself, parts she'd thought to be dreams, and bequeathed them to Rio, to Marcos, to the relief units, and to her jobs. In the end, there was only enough left to turn back home.

She was already in the front yard when she heard the shooting. She ran toward the gunshots.

Beckerfield's gates were opened, the huge walls covered with golf players looming over her. Their way of saying that this wasn't her place, even if it was her hometown.

More shots. The back of her head screamed. *Go away. This is not what you need now.*

Alzira crossed through to the entrance house and hopped up across the musty furniture clustered there. Her legs brushed the overgrown foliage when she exited the other side.

Three people ran deeper into the field, each clad in black. At four different points, she saw something...someone erupting from the ground, scattering fresh brown dirt.

A bush shook a few steps from her.

"Alzira... Go away."

Alfredo. Hurt, hiding...

"It was a trap..." His ecobag was toppled beside him, buds spreading over the soil. "You have nothing to do with us..."

"It wasn't me who came into your life," she said, hands trembling, lips quivering. "You're... hurt. Can you stand?" Blood expanded over his shirt above the waist.

"The pigs shot us... They were hidden. They got Gui..."

She hoisted Alfredo up and passed an arm around his shoulders. He limped forward. She glanced behind her, but there was no sign of the skull pigs.

"They might've killed Gui," Alfredo groaned while she forced him toward the golf course's entrance. "I saw him falling. I promised I'd give him a new computer to watch classes. Damn, why can't I fulfill anything in this life? Please, tell my aunt I was going to visit... Let me just remember her number. It's—"

"You won't die." Alzira pulled him quickly across the junk in the abandoned entrance. He was crying. She was too.

They trudged along the street, back to her home, to Mami's place. From the moment she crossed Beckerfield's gates, she didn't look back. More shots were fired in the distance, but she wouldn't look. There was no reason to look back.

A crowd of evacuees was entering the course. Eyes curious, voices raising.

"It's for you," Alfredo said to them as they passed. "Go get them, make a fuss. Alzira—" He turned to her, breath clipped.

"What?" She said, not looking at him. "Be still, please."

"I remembered the word I tried to say back then..." he whispered. "The cheese in the baião left it more... home-made. It made me feel as if I belonged, which I haven't felt since I left Aunt Alícia."

She nodded and paced along the street, leaving behind the shouting people, certain of their voices rising.

People gathered around the dollhouse Jota had planted on a patch of turf between two sprouses. They'd never seen the miniature kind, though the most skilled knew it could be made. He never wanted to show that to anyone before. His mother hadn't taught the people about the tiny house she'd first seen planted in her own backyard—and that stayed there until Jota was a teenager. *Not the time*, she used to say. *People will only want to sell them like Aramá souvenirs.* But now it was the time. He'd heard about communities planting sprouses in Rio Preto, Volta Redonda, and even in the leveled parts of Rio de Janeiro. Inevitable days had arrived.

"So Grandpa and Uncle Guilherme fled..." Célia said, helping the boy wind the June party flags around the dollhouse.

"Yes. Uncle Guilherme hurt his arm but escaped. He managed to plant a bud between him and the squad. And Grandma... She hid Grandpa from the authorities. But once the people entered Beckerfield... There are things that work like trees... Like sprouses... There was no turning back."

Alzira sank a trowel into the soil and dug a chunk off it. She carefully placed a bud in the hole and covered it with earth. She tapped an icon on her tablet. All around her, other residents were doing the same, planting the seeds of home.

Not all storms were meant to be contained by her, Mami had reminded her when she first thought of returning home months before she passed away. But some were meant to be stirred by her.

DIFFERENT KINDS OF DEFIANCE

This is one of the two flash fictions in this collection, and the one that gives it its name. Like in "Even Though You're No More" (the other flash fiction), here we're also in a post-apocalyptic world. The world in this one is suffering with extreme desertification, but finally finding its way out of it through an ingenious technology of transporting trees from one place to the other, along with the capacity to recreate their invisible structures of roots and mycelia underground. It's a brief story about change, newness, and the movements of life.

This one was written for a contest in a writing group in early 2021 with the theme "two storms." I thought of two meanings for "storm," one positive and one negative. Here, the first storm was the one that ravaged the world, an unnamed climate catastrophe caused by humankind that turned lands and forests into desert and dwindled humanity's capacity for survival. But the second storm is the one that's yet to come, and this one will be positive, a storm caused by the hands of those resisting and surviving, doing something to get out of the bad times and to avoid even worse times. That's why this story pairs very well with the previous one, "Soil of Our Home, Storm of Our Lives," since the positive meaning for the word "storm" is also there. And it's also fitting for the title of this collection, since in every story you're reading (or have read) here, you'll find different kinds of defiance, from planting a tree to stirring a revolution.

· · ● · ● · ● · · ·

Is it too late to pray for a second storm?

I was a little girl when my grandpa told me that to have healthy leaves, you first need healthy soil. And I'm an old, grieving climate engineer when I show my granddaughter I'm disfiguring the woodlands close to our home.

"You're yanking off our trees, Granny..." Julia crosses her arms, a wrinkle of heartbreak on her lips. Oh, yeah, she's right. With a simple tap on my pad, a group of seven trees rips out of the soil of what we call our Backyard Forest. The rings around their trunks switch on, air thrusters activating. The roots drip sap as the trees position themselves on the soil-drones floating nearby.

"It's for a good reason." The soil-drones' edges gleam

in blue as the roots cohere with the drone's medium. The Backyard Forest is where my beloved Emily and I laid our offerings and prayed for better tidings, where we terraformed—terra-healed—our first river and collected fresh water from a grotto to nourish our saplings. And where I lost my lovely Emily to the first storm. But today, after years of love and cultivation, that place is also a lush extravaganza: a sanctuary in a world in need of oases. "Besides, what did I say about the Backyard Forest, Ju?"

"It's not ours."

"Why?"

"Flags can't be stuck on the soil."

I wave a finger. "Never."

More soil-drones glide down, and the tree rings light up. More roots pulled out, more trees hovering and replanting themselves on the drones. I touch the pad, and one of the drones comes to us, a bigger one for sturdier trees.

"What about flying?" I ask, wheeling our luggage and resting it on a soil-drone.

"Can we?" Oh, those hazelnut eyes glistening in the unwavering sunlight...

We hop on the drone. I fasten our legs and waists to the strap system, clenching my teeth to ignore the pains in my leg and belly. In minutes, we're leaving home and wafting with our Backyard Forest all around us, hundreds of trees dislocated from their bedding for the first time.

"Why is our home different?" Julia asks as we fly and leave the rim of the terra-healed lands Emily and I projected. She gapes down at the wastelands that span all around. Canyons that once caroled with water; lands thrummed by drought; villages and ruins wrecked by a storm are now silent.

"When I met your Grannie Emily, our home was not

unlike all of this."

Julia dares to look behind.

"Granny... our Forest..." She's crying. I drape an arm around her shoulders. "It's gone." Our solitary house lies naked in our reserve, except for the copse where the family tombstones are located—Emily's and Josh's, Julia's father.

I speak the next words with a lump in my throat.

"Our Backyard Forest is needed somewhere else, sweetie." The Forest's where she learned to walk, where she planted her first seeds and said goodbye to Josh. It can't be easy to see it scattered. It isn't for me.

We start to descend toward the refugee tents and shanties. Hundreds of thousands of them are scattered across the wastelands of absolute climate collapse. The shred of a river cuts the camp like a scar, threatening to extinguish itself. Tired eyes stare up, calloused hands pointing at the forest that descends from the skies. My soil-drones spread, detecting the best spots to position their nutrient-packed modules.

Julia gapes at the roots as they wriggle out of the soil-drones' bases and stick to the bister-painted land that longs to be green. She turns back at my grimace.

"Are you in pain, Granny?"

"It's those old bones of mine, sweetie."

Our soil-drone lands with a soft thud. Julia grabs my hand as we hop off. A woman approaches to greet us, peppering Ladybugs on the soil from a basket in her hands. One day, Emily came to me like that: a tired, thirsty wanderer, but with a boy in her arms instead of soil-harmonizing tiny bots.

"Ju, this is Akpena, our new friend. We'll spend some time here."

Akpena smiles and shakes Julia's hand. It warms my heart that Julia smiles back because she'll see that face a lot in the coming years. Her eyes gleam when some Ladybugs shine in red and drill holes into the dry land while the warm wind scatters other ones.

"Is the soil ready for coupling?" I say. "Synth-mycelium, nutrients, and everything else?"

"Half of it is done," Akpena says, her eyes not evading from my Ju.

I kneel before my granddaughter, joints protesting.

"You're now part of a storm too, Ju."

"I don't want to do it. You always said we need to be defiant."

"Ju, sweetie, there are different kinds of defiance."

I hug her and close my eyes. Even if I can't be part of it, I pray for the storm that will breed around the world from all the camps like that one. A storm of healing and blooming and granddaughters with futures.

ANTICIPATION OF HOLLOWNESS

This was my first Solarpunk story when I still didn't know what exactly was Solarpunk. This is also my story that traveled the farthest until now. At the time of writing, it was published in English (text and audio), Italian (text, audio, and comics), Portuguese, and a Chinese translation is on the way.

This story came about when I imagined a "perfect" city. Everything works, everything is sustainable, and almost everyone seems reasonably satisfied with the world. It looks like an utopian city. I try to convey that in the story through the descriptions, the architecture, and the way some characters behave.

The contrast comes in Janet's relationship with her city and in the memories of her aunt. It is through Janet's existence that we learn Sundyal is an utopia, but not for everyone. I don't remember who exactly first said that, but "one's utopia is another's dystopia." This is an idea I think about since I started writing. My first (poor) attempt at writing science fiction, in 2011, came from that idea—it was a story about a city created to unknowingly preserve the interests of a wealthy planet's elite. And you'll find this idea again and see it through an even bleaker lens in "To Remember the Poison," a novelette first published in this collection.

• • • • ● • ● • • •

Having an obsolete best friend meant I had to put up with constant warnings about her plight. "Software needs to be updated," Lyria said and stopped abruptly on our way to the Algae on Wheels. Her hands slumped and stiffened against her sides. "Software will shut down unless updated." A few meters ahead, the floating algaewich rickshaw honked twice, announcing its imminent departure.

"Well, Lyria," I said, chuckling, "you're way too predictable. Have I told you?" I waved to Roberto, the algaewich vendor. He was gliding the rickshaw away across the street. Its buffed surface reflected the rosy skies giving way to the darkness of night. Roberto flashed a wide smile when he saw me. He steered the Algae on Wheels into a parking area designated for bicycles, rickshaws, and the like.

"Janet, about predictability, I would like to—"

"Shush, friend. There's our man."

I ran. Lyria followed me as she always did. Her feet clanked unevenly on the asphalt.

It tastes like algae, but it's hidden among slices of bread! advertised a small hologram floating in blue and yellow around the roof of the Algae on Wheels, sometimes crossing through the round solar panel on it.

Lyria tried to keep up with me, but her legs were old, marred by time and use, unable to run without making her look like an unwieldy dancer. Nothing about her age was new for me. Her alerts had been warning me about her obsolescence for more than two years.

The mucky scent of algae struck us before we approached Algae on Wheels' serving hatch.

"It's the best algaewich in all of Sundyal," Roberto told us. A rehearsed approach, though his eyes gleamed as if he was revealing a secret.

"You say that every day, Roberto," I said. "I'm always around."

"Oh!" Roberto smirked, flinging a spatula around in his hand. Bread falling on algae falling on bread sizzling on the grill. "Standard algaewich?"

I nodded. The algae and bread mixture hissed. My stomach rumbled, rioting for the lack of other options.

"I'm not good with faces," Roberto said. "Though that one is hard to forget." He indicated toward Lyria with his chin.

She stood impassive next to me, waiting with her hands tight against her sides. The wind ruffled the few strands of the plastic fiber hair that remained on her head, threads of her past. Flaps of skin peeled off her jaw. She blinked her orange eyes with no pupils, some lines on her face twitching in a spasm.

Outdated hardware and software caused a lot of problems with Lyria's structure. She twitched, sometimes bent to one side, tilted her head involuntarily, and uttered unintelligible sentences. Her biografted skin was a lot older than that of the smooth androids that weaved their way seamlessly amidst the humans in Sundyal. The modern kind was beautiful and advanced but more humdrum than Lyria and loaded with repetitive sentences tuned for their specific functions.

"She's easy to spot," I said, smiling to Lyria.

"I'm easy to spot," Lyria concurred. "I am a walking ad." She put a hand on her chest, above the fading casino ad on it. *Celebrate Mendolowski Day with 10,000 specoins in prizes, you lucky duck!* On her belly, only the golden beak of a duck remained.

"That casino doesn't even exist anymore," I said. "Her software is outdated, she still struggles to remember some things."

Roberto laughed, packing my algaewich in a pasteboard wrapping. The swampy odor wafted up to my nose.

"How much?" I straightened my glasses.

Roberto curled his thumb in the air above his accounting pad. A tiny hologram drifted up from it. "It will be 3 specoins."

"Oh, crap." I glanced at Lyria.

"What's wrong?" Roberto frowned.

"She's my wallet too." I turned to my friend, clasping her hands. "Please, tell me good news, dear."

"This price is not recommended," Lyria said, her brows jerking in what might have been a worried expression in her up-to-date, blackjack dealer past. "It is best for you to not spend this money."

I sighed. I wouldn't know what to do without her—what I

would have to do eventually because her software had an expiration date. I shivered at the thought. In Sundyal, non-expiring stuff ended up with well-off folks. For women like me, not a recipient of a wealthy heritage or large dividends, only finite stuff was left to reap.

"You can wait a little bit." Roberto shrugged. "I'm used to that. Early evening, people have left work a while ago, gone home to their comfy beds. The streets are almost empty now." He opened his arms. "Prices will go down."

"How much time?" I said. "I need to eat, and if I don't eat now there won't be anywhere I can eat till tomorrow." *Anywhere with a reasonable price for a girl that didn't fit*, I thought but decided not to say aloud.

"Well... look!" The man zoomed in on the price tag hologram. "Two specoins."

"Still not recommended," said Lyria.

"Aw, snap. Pay him."

"One coin!" Roberto spread his arms like a magician reaching the finale of a trick. He picked up the algaewich and handed it to me. "Buy it now. If partiers or tourists swarm by it will go up. If they're lucky in the casinos tonight I could bet on 6 specoins."

"Buy it!" I stroke Lyria's side. "Buy it, buy it!"

"Transferring," Lyria said. A ping sounded on Roberto's pad. "Transferred."

"It was a pleasure doing business with you, young lady," Roberto said, blinking and starting the rickshaw. Its thrusters whirred and propelled it forward. "I'll try to recall your face next time." The Algae on Wheels dinged twice.

I nodded and chomped my algaewich. My stomach demanded it.

Lyria and I strolled along Caravana Street. Dronelights lit

the way, faintly buzzing above our heads. Dustbots skimmed the ground, sucking in dust from the already excessively clean pavement. The closed businesses and the light leaking from the apartments in the two-story buildings with solar-paneled roofs were on my path home every day. I used to rove around Sundyal, sometimes aimlessly, sometimes in search of good music, beautiful paintings, free stuff to do, and quiet spots to have insightful chats with Lyria.

"How is the algaewich, Janet?"

"Nasty as always, but my belly finds it pleasing."

A hurrah echoed, coming from a casino down the street. A group of women in colorful maxi dresses laughed, gossiped, and bragged about something that probably involved specoins. Just a few steps from them, a group of men wearing similarly smart dark suits and distinct tie colors did the same.

"What do you think about us testing our luck?" I said.

"Luck is not meant to be tested, but enjoyed."

"Is that one of the lines you told blackjack players?" I licked my lips and took another bite of the algaewich.

"I used to end with, 'Enjoy your luck and bet more.'"

"And they did. And they lost."

"Of course. The house always—"

Lyria halted. Part of our days. I closed my eyes and exhaled, gritting my teeth. From someone's apartment, a guitar wept.

"Software needs to be updated," Lyria said. "Software will shut down unless it's updated."

"Oh, will it shut down?" I pivoted to stand in front of Lyria, defying her, full of scorn, glaring at the damp orange orbits of her eyes. "Will it?"

"It will, indeed."

"You know what? Show me the Solartop menu." I tucked my glasses back in place.

"I must recommend caution," Lyria said, almost as mechanically as she had professed her own death sentence seconds before, electronic feedback coming out of her speakers and distorting her voice. "Solartop is the most expensive restaurant in Sundyal. Your current balance is 25 specoins."

"That's why I wanna check it out. Come on." I gestured to hurry her. "I'm not forcing you to show me anything, but if you don't, I'll go there myself and check it." I pointed to the red beam of light that emanated from the city center and got lost in the sky. It originated from Solartop.

Lyria projected the menu on the pavement. "There it is, Janet." That was one of the amazing things about Lyria. I could be pissed off, but she never was. She was always a good listener—and a good advisor, prompt with info, who often monopolized all reason and prudence in our relationship. "Solartop's prices are fixed."

I read the menu aloud, "Hauckländer soy sausage dipped in pepper and Frödzan printed cheese. Well, 95 specoins. So, no. Salty waffles with olives. 94. Fufu Fafa Fefe. What even is that? Well, this one is way off anyway. 345. Algae-packed shrimp." I tapped my foot on the pavement, indicating toward the menu. "Do you see it, Lyria? Of course, you do. These algae find their place everywhere."

My eyes rolled down the menu, disregarding almost everything on it. Solartop was way out of my league. It was a three-story building in central Sundyal, the *only* building that was allowed to maintain more than two stories. It was the beacon of a sustainable world that left behind skyscrapers, most automobiles, and the hustle n' bustle, blind-to-the-environment way of life. Three days before Aunt Monica passed away, she'd promised to take me there. *The place is full of history*, she'd said, ripping the laminated paper wrapped around a temaki and splitting it with me.

"Here it is!" I spotted an item and put a foot over it. "Speckles of syrupy carrot. And it's just 20 specoins."

"What is that?"

I roared with laughter, and it echoed through the moonless night of Caravana Street. Someone protested, but I didn't care.

"I have no idea, but we'll have it tomorrow. Let's toast to our friendship."

"How is that done?"

"We'll sit there and we'll talk and we'll eat—well, I'll eat, you'll watch—expensive food that won't sate my hunger, then I'll drop my remaining cash on the Algae on Wheels to fill my belly. Sound like a plan?"

"Sounds like a problem."

I stood on tiptoe and draped an arm across Lyria's shoulders. She was a few inches taller than me. "It isn't. I want to have this special dinner with you, my only friend. So, tomorrow night, we'll dine at the top of the world."

I rushed forward, leaving Lyria steps behind me. I didn't want her to see the tears beading on my eyes. She wouldn't feel sorry for me, but she could ask what this *intensity* was that I was feeling. She often felt curious enough to save data about humans in her corrupted files and databases. I knew that one day Lyria would shut herself down, close her orange eyes forever, and leave me alone and empty. The only words I had to describe the feeling were "*anticipation of hollowness*". She wouldn't get it.

"What do you think, Lyria?" I held a heart-checkered black dress in front of me by its shoulders and moved it under a lamp protruding out of the wall above my mattress. The details stood out, stains of Aunt Monica's life, a rebellious thread, and small holes like chasms of time. "Does it fit?"

Lyria ambled from the space I liked to call my living room, though it had only a table, a set of chairs fixed with shims, broken dronelights, and a refrigerator repurposed as a wardrobe.

"I think the best way to discover if it fits is by trying it on," Lyria said. I fancied her blunt truth. Humans should be just like her. It would all be so much easier.

"Well, my aunt was stronger than me in all sorts of ways. I don't know if it would fit well." I brushed away two moths from the dress.

"Why don't you try?"

I eyed the dress from top down. The only person I could picture inside it was Aunt Monica. How many times had her high heels clicked the uneven steps of our basement? Six times a week, minimum. She arrived from her friend Samantha's place and stood at the foot of the stairs with that sheath dress. From a distance, the white hearts on black looked like small circles for a nearsighted girl like me. At those moments, Aunt Monica usually broke down singing with a hoarse voice. Either that or she blared, "Breaking News! Breaking right now!" And then she would hop right into a story about a woman who donated all her money to sustainability projects or about that other one who arrived in a casino wearing fox fur and was awash with boos and aggressive accusations.

Aunt Monica used to chortle and dance in the darkness of the basement lit only by old-fashioned lanterns and uneven candlelights. She'd always been in tune with Sundyal, even if we didn't belong. So long as the wine hadn't brought her down, our house had been full of joy and noise and exaggerated gossip.

"Do I deserve to wear it?" I said to Lyria, my attention returning to the outfit.

"I do not understand the conditions of merit about this dress." Lyria analyzed it with her single-colored eyes vibrating behind their sockets. Of course, she wouldn't understand. Nobody but me could still hear the loud voice of Aunt Monica reverberating through the stones of the basement, her tears forming seas of smeared makeup.

I won't go away. Aunt Monica was wearing that same dress when she let it all out. *I know I don't have an education, I don't have the—how do they say it?—the capacity, I can't even sort out how to throw my trash in the right colored bins. But I was born here, I've seen the end of changes in this sustainability fad, the last skyscrapers converted into these buildings the size of damned teddy bears. That's not how you solve a problem, you can't do it by just running over other problems, recommending that people like me go to faraway cities, dislodging thousands. I won't go!*

Lyria put a hand on my shoulder and woke me up from the past.

"You are silent," she said. "Humans are rarely silent."

I placed the dress on my mattress. "Do you think I'll have to go away when you... shut down?"

"Why would you have to go away?"

"I don't belong here. This place is for intelligent people, rich artists, students, entrepreneurs, high-skilled casino players. This is a city for the aristocracy. I can't even find a job serving them. I'm draining the remainder of Aunt Monica's coffers with your budgetary help. I couldn't live here without you. It just wouldn't work."

"Why not?" Lyria gawked at me. Once, I found her face

funny with all the flapping skin and her crooked chin, a shabby girl out of someone else's trash, but now I felt nothing but affection for that android. I wished I could repair her, if not update her to a newer version, then replace her parts with the first-class, sustainable biografts that were top of the line in Sundyal.

"You're my wallet, you're my guide here, I don't have smart devices and wearable stuff. I can't deal with Sundyal without you being a sort of... interface?"

"You could make some other friends."

"It's just that—" I slid a finger over Aunt Monica's dress. "If I wear this, I feel like I'll have to fight for my place here."

"I thought you already did that every day." Lyria picked up the dress, but it fell on the floor when she raised her arm.

She stopped in her usual position, arms swinging like pendulums.

"Software needs to be updated. Software will shut down unless updated."

I scooped the dress up and brushed the dust from it.

The mirrored elevator door at the end of the Solartop building's main foyer shunned my gaze from it. I was slim, Aunt Monica was not, so the dress sagged a bit against my body. I wore glasses, but she didn't. Yet, I visualized her inside the dress.

I'd brought a frayed wristlet clutch bag that matched my dress. I knew that the kind of women who attended Solartop used to carry them, so I stuffed mine with crumpled paper to make it look like a legitimate one. I also wore a pair of wooden upper clogs. I didn't have the magic feet of my aunt, capable of being supported by high heels without losing her charm.

"Look at these walls," I whispered to Lyria, snickering. "We're gonna spend all my money." Tapestries covered the walls on the route to the elevator. One depicted a woman with gritted teeth plucking out a skyscraper from the ground beneath her. Another one showed the same muscular woman holding the sun in her hands. Aunt Monica had told me the story of Olivia Mendolowski, the woman who had changed the face of Sundyal.

A maître d' popped out of nowhere, appearing suddenly from behind me.

"These are handwoven, ma'am." He looked at Lyria. "Madams." I had tried to work on Lyria's appearance. I'd cut off any peeling skin, had hidden her chest ad with a coat of yellow paint, and performed all kinds of touch-ups to try to make her blend in better with Solartop's usual clientele. She was still far off.

I didn't know what to say to the maitre d'. He had smooth, lustrous cheeks. His eyes were green, and his thin mustache gleamed with wax.

"They tell the story of Olivia Mendolowski, the woman who crushed down the old ways, the pollution, the waste and raised Sundyal from a languishing city. You two must be quite well versed in her doings, but I find it appropriate to explain since you showed an interest in our tapestries."

"They're gorgeous," I said, for lack of a better term.

"Printed replicas are available for just 180 specoins. You—"

"We have a reservation, please. My name's Janet."

"Right away, ma'am." He stood upright, and his eyes glinted blue.

I elbowed Lyria and whispered, "He's an android! What skin. He has perfect movements. Did you see it?"

"Should I feel what you call jealousy?"

"It's envy. You want to be like him, so it's envy."

"No." Lyria elbowed me back. "I am worried you might pick him as a new friend. So it is jealousy. Am I right?"

I laughed out loud, then muffled my guffaws when a couple of women glanced over and narrowed their eyes. They carried clutch bags that seemed emptier than mine.

"We have set your table," said the maître d'. "Please, follow me."

The man ushered us to the elevator, a moving, self-contained palace featuring paintings of Olivia Mendolowski signing some paperwork, demolishing a factory, and brandishing a solar panel like a shield. A golden orbed lamp floated above our heads, no wire connecting it to anything.

"Olivia Mendolowski used this very building to gather her faithful workers and devise a new world of sustainability and equity." *Swiftly and politically relocating the poor populace,* I thought to myself without voicing it. "That's the reason this is the only structure in Sundyal allowed to have three stories."

The elevator dinged on the third and top floor.

"Wow..." My mouth hung open.

I drowned in clinking cutlery, the crooning of educated voices, and a soft violin melody weaving through the air. Floating chandeliers with intricate ornaments of pearl and gold hovered above the tables. Flowers with their stems curling around a candle floated above each napkin holder. Frames were hung on the blue wall, exhibiting faces with excessive mustaches, beards, hats, suits, and even a man with a parrot on his head. The only person I recognized was Olivia Mendolowski herself.

"It's fantastic, Lyria."

I'd never been in a place so exquisitely decorated. Aunt Monica once took me to Samantha's apartment. Up until now, her place had had the most beautiful assortment of furniture and style I'd ever seen. It was there that I'd discovered Samantha paid 5 specoins for Aunt Monica to clean and brush away every inch of dirt. My aunt used to say with a little hubris that she had the last blue-collar job in Sundyal.

The maître d' slightly bowed before us. He seemed to be always slightly bowing. "Please, accompany me."

We followed the android. The red light that glowed into the night sky of Sundyal came from a pillar in the center of Solartop, etched with the gleaming outlines of skyscrapers crumbling down. Beyond the initial area, I'd stepped into, a terrace stretched out with more tables and a view of the two-story world down below. *The teddy bears.*

The maître d' guided us to a central table, pulling out the chairs for us to sit. I shivered. I wasn't that important. Who was I to be there in the middle, like a centerpiece? I was just a poor girl, a status quo leftover accompanied by a flaking android.

"This is so… out of my world."

"It is located in your world, Janet," Lyria said. Her body teetered to the left when she sat.

"That's the irony, isn't it? It's been right here this whole time. My world. My city."

A waiter's impassive face appeared beside me, his smile stretching from ear to ear. Another android. "Can I take your orders, madams?"

I mumbled, the words stuck in my throat.

"May I suggest our Fufu Fafa Fefe?" The android opened his hands. A gelatinous puddle showed up in a hologram. "It's the only one awarded five stars in all of Sundyal. It goes well with Thelesian wine, vintage 2099."

I leaned toward Lyria. "Is there more than one place serving these Fufu thingies?" I suppressed a laugh. Solartop seemed the kind of place that wouldn't condone my kind of laughter. An unwavering smile persisted on the waiter's face.

"I'd like to—I mean—my order is..." I scratched my head, trying to remember the odd name of the carrot food. "I forgot it, damn. Oh, pardon my language. I—"

"Speckles of syrupy carrot." Lyria saved me. "We would like that."

"So, two speckles?" The Fufu stuff disappeared from the waiter's hand, and he produced a tablet from his apron.

"No!" I bit my lip, realizing I was speaking too loudly. "No, please. Just one. My friend... she is an android. Bring just an empty plate for her, will you?"

"Of course. What would you like to drink?"

"I'd like wine. Beer. Vodka. But I won't. Just the carrot thing, please."

"No problem, madam."

The waiter walked into the kitchen with an elegant stride, his hands behind his back.

"This place is surreal," I said, glancing around. "Look at these people..."

That sounded like an invitation. Lyria's head swiveled to peek around, almost performing a full circle.

Two stylish women chatted while gesturing gleefully. A robust man with dreadlocks took mouthfuls of the Fufu stuff, occasionally sipping a glass of a green drink. I'd seen him before on the news, some kind of casino owner. In the terrace, a woman that resembled Samantha nodded to a man who seemed to talk a lot. Next to the kitchen entrance, a brazen-bearded man in a tweed coat fidgeted with chopsticks to eat some wormlike food. On the other side of his table, a girl chuckled and slapped at a hologram game on a tablet.

I inhaled, closing my eyes for a few seconds. "So, Lyria, now that I've taken it all in, let's celebrate our friendship."

"You said something about sitting, talking, and eating. Should we wait for your food?"

"No, the celebrations can start now." I raised an empty glass of wine. "Do the same. Please, don't break it."

Lyria raised her glass.

"To our friendship," I said. "Now, repeat."

"To our friendship."

"That was nice." I carefully placed the glass back down, rested my elbows on the table, and smiled. "I never thought the number 4,324 would mean so much for me. I'm going to tell you something I never did."

"Please, do."

"When that seller said I was visitor number 4,324 and gave me you as a gift, I knew he was getting rid of his trash."

"Are you calling me trash?" Lyria tilted her head. She was trying to make a joke.

"*His* trash. One person's trash is another's treasure. Isn't that a slogan of some recycling company?"

"Are you calling me a treasure?"

"Sort of. But that's not what I wanted to tell you. I was in that man's shop to steal. I wasn't hungry, but I saw a sparkling candy that drove me crazy. I just wanted that stuff. It said it would pop inside my mouth." I laughed. "I was just an... obsolete fifteen-year-old girl. I didn't know these things even existed. Am I right? Stuff that just pops *inside* your mouth. Who wouldn't want it? So, I wished to grab it. Instead, I came out of that shop with you tagging along."

"Am I your bargaining chip for sparkling candy?"

"It depends. If you don't update yourself, you may very well be."

"You know I cannot—"

"Stop. I know." My shoulders slumped. Anticipation of hollowness. I'd never felt that even when Aunt Monica told me day after day that she wouldn't last, that she had a disease, that life was brittle for the ones who didn't belong. "Lyria, tell me something I don't know. Something about you. Surprise me. Dig deep into those stone-age databases."

Lyria stared at me as if she were mulling over my words. I knew she couldn't do that. Mulling over in her mind was called processing.

"While working at casinos, I used to broadcast a radio station that played old songs," Lyria said. "An old lady gambler once called me Lyria because of that; she said I had plenty of romantic lyrics to offer to her broken heart."

"You!" I crossed my arms across my chest. "You never told me that before and you have never broadcast anything for me." I understood how Lyria worked. Aunt Monica had taught me over algaewiches and temakis everything she had known about basic programming and artificial intelligence. And yet I was still surprised by how my friend expressed her thoughts and quasi-feelings.

"I cannot anymore. My music module is obsolete."

"Madams, excuse me." The smooth waiter put the plate with the carrot stuff in front of me and an empty plate in front of Lyria. "*Bon appétit!*"

I glowered at my plate. I would flush all my cash away on that thing. "They should call it little balls of carrot with oil. Whatever."

The first bite seemed like eating paper. With the second little ball I couldn't decide whether it was salty or sweet. It was only on the third bite that I realized it was better than algaewiches, but not almost 20 specoins better.

"Dad! Look at this lady."

I gulped. The girl that had been playing the hologram game was gaping at Lyria. Her eyes reflected the crimson of Solartop's central pillar. She looked about nine years old.

"Her name is Lyria," I said, smiling. "Tell Lyria your name."

Lyria's head swiveled to face the girl, and for a moment, I feared the odd angle of my friend's head would frighten her. It didn't.

"My name is Aadab."

"Hi, Aadab," Lyria said. "My name is Lyria."

"I know." The girl chuckled. Like a protector shadow, her father watched from a distance, hands in his pockets, one more bearded man between two others in the hanging frames. When our gazes met, he blinked.

"Do you play games?" Aadab asked, jigging and clapping her hands. "You're one of the old casino models, aren't you?"

"How do you know that?" I frowned. It wasn't typical for a girl her age to know about casino androids.

"My dad works with the new models." She pivoted her head to face her father. "Don't you, Dad? But he doesn't let me play with them. He says work is work."

"I am retired, Aadab," said Lyria. "I can play with you."

"She wants to play with me, Dad." Aadab turned to her father, who still didn't move from his watching position. He nodded.

Lyria raised her left hand, palm front. "Tap my right hand."

Aadab tapped her left. "Oh!"

"You lose." Lyria's hand moved to her forehead. "Tap my

nape."

The little girl clenched her teeth, turned around Lyria's chair, and scored, chuckling throughout. This time, I was the one agape. Her joviality impressed me in a way I didn't think possible. At her age, I was just an uneasy girl waiting for an aunt to come home and bring pieces of food, jokes, and gossip. I had my games to play, but I played them feeling a trepidation inside me, like some kind of alarm that was about to ring but never did.

Lyria lifted three fingers. "Quick! Show me four fingers like these!"

The girl showed four and scored again.

"You're good, Aadab," Lyria said. "I am impressed."

"I am too." Aadab's father came out of the shadows and patted his daughter's head, his thick beard contorting to reveal a smile. "The old models are outstanding. MX-CSN-10294, isn't it?"

"I—" I'd never thought about Lyria's model before.

"I am," she said.

"Almost a decade without updates." The man put his hands on his daughter's shoulders. She stared at Lyria and now stretched her little fingers out to touch the few remaining fibers on my friend's head. "I'm curious as to where you found her. It's not forbidden to have one, but it is to build one like her. It doesn't follow the MGS."

I raised an eyebrow.

"I mean, Mendolowski's Guidelines of Sustainability. Also, this MX-CSN is one of the last casino models with the capacity for acquiring certain human behaviors unrelated to her trade. The new models are less prone to error, but they don't simulate emotions like Lyria. It's not even coded in them."

"I don't think she *simulates* emotions," I said, folding my arms, swallowing the truth I didn't want to hear.

"I'm sorry." The man shook his head. "I can be quite technical at times. It wasn't my intention to jeopardize your evening. By the way, my name is Mohammed."

"Janet." I couldn't be drier. My eyes turned aside to the carrot stuff. I'd trade it for algaewiches any time now.

"Hi, Mohammed. I am Lyria."

"Pleased to meet both of you."

I moved my head, trying to put a smile on my face.

"I won't bother you anymore," Mohammed said, clasping his little girl's hand. Now she gawked at the distant and tall face of her father. "But I wanted to—how can I put this?—I wanted to ask you if you could lend me your friend indefinitely for a considerable sum of specoins? Do you think you could be happy with 4,000?"

"What? Are you offering to buy Lyria?" I pushed back my chair. It scratched the floor. People glared at us. The dreadlocked man from the news lifted his head from his Fufu. Some noises and behaviors didn't fit in this building that represented the future. I was a relic from the past simmering there.

"I can give her a full refurbishment. New hair, new limbs, a new set of eyes. I can make her look almost human. Like those men." He pointed to one of the waiters that carried a tray of overpriced shrimp in one hand. "Would you like it, Lyria?" He turned his gaze from me to Lyria.

My heart thudded, and the hair on my arms bristled in anger. I wanted to drag his gaze back to me. I lowered a heavy hand onto the table. The glasses and plates clinked.

Lyria turned her face to me, then to Mohammed. "It would be really—"

"Nasty." I stood. Aadab blinked and took a few steps back. "It would be really nasty. Could I make an offer on one of your friends, perhaps?"

Mohammed blushed. At first, I thought he was angry, but then I realized it was shame.

"I'm sorry," he stuttered. "I'm really sorry, Janet."

"Don't call me that. Call me Miss or something else."

"I didn't mean to offend. I—I—" Aadab pulled his hand. "I must go."

They wandered back to their table.

I propped my elbows on the table, took off my glasses, and tried to hide my tears from Lyria. My night of celebration, my once-in-a-lifetime event, my toast to friendship, had been ruined by a man with a disproportionate offer. It seemed that up there at the top there was always a proposition to bring you down, back to your place, to where you belonged.

"Would you like a glass of wine, ma'am?" The smooth-faced waiter woke me from my thoughts. I moved my hands away from my eyes, put my glasses back on, and Solartop regained its colors around me. The diners' attention had diverted back to their meals. The couple with clutch bags had replaced the dreadlocked man.

"No."

The waiter nodded and glided toward another table. On Mohammed's, Aadab had resumed her game, but now without so much as a titter. Her father stared at nothing, his gaze lost, pensive.

"I'm sorry, Lyria. I should've asked for your opinion in all this."

"There is nothing to be sorry about, Janet. We are celebrating. Sit, talk, and eat, you told me. We are fulfilling all those conditions, though you have not touched the speckles of syrupy carrot for a while now."

I smiled. If it had been minutes before, I'd be bothering Solartop's clientele with my laughter.

"How rude of Mohammed," I said. "You don't offer to buy people's friends." But what should I have expected, coming to Solartop, home of Sundyal's vanguard, cradle of the future? What should Aunt Monica have expected working for Samantha? When she staggered down the stairs of our basement shrieking the news, she'd been drunk and laughing with one of her high heels broken, her make-up a fuzzy mess, but the temaki intact in her hand.

"That woman invited me to live in her apartment," Aunt Monica had said. "With all her luxuries, all her booze. Oh, dear Jan, who does she think I am? Some kind of monster?"

"We can go there," I said, open to the possibility of living in a place where sunlight filtered through electronic shutters. "Why not, Aunt?"

"Oh, girl. It's no place for us."

It had been all she'd said before snoring herself to sleep, but I knew there was something deeper. Months later, at my aunt's memorial, Samantha told me she'd offered a good life to Monica. If only she'd accepted, if only things had been different. I could even have visited my aunt whenever I wished.

That had struck me down, and a bad day had turned into a crumbling one. My legs had become frail, and I'd walked away from the memorial before it had ended, still hearing Aunt Monica's laughter, her trampling on the stairs, still smelling temaki with salmon and chive.

"What is bothering you?" Lyria placed her hand over mine. Her fragile hair was tossed over her eyes.

"You're not a simulation to me." The word sounded like acid on my lips. "So, I should've treated you like a person. But I treated you the same way Mohammed did. I'm sorry, Lyria."

"Please, explain."

"Your opinion. I want it. Would you happily accept Mohammed's offer? He could give you a new body, a new mind, he could make you like these fluffy waiters. You would be his, and—"

Lyria sat upright. "Software needs to be updated. Software will shut down unless updated."

"I know, I know. Now, please, tell me what you think."

"Shutting down..."

"What? No!" I leaned over the table, grasping Lyria's hands. Her eyes rolled on their orbits and shut tight. My arm knocked the empty wineglass to the floor. It shattered. The floating flowers curled around the candle were next, but they just drifted away in a straight line, the flame perishing. One of the waiters caught the decoration, and another one was already cleaning up my mess.

"Lyria!"

People stared at us, giving accusatory glares of non-belonging. My belly churned in pain. Lyria's head tilted back as if she was merely sleeping, a drunken android, tired of bullshit, tired of being the only one.

I kneeled before Lyria and opened the panel door in her neck. Oily wires and a switched-off terminal slid out. What would I do with that? My teeth were clenched together, and in between them, I repeated, "Lyria, Lyria, Lyria," as if those were the magical words that would bring her back.

A hand landed on my shoulder.

"It won't work, my friend."

Mohammed.

"Go away!" If he hadn't popped out of his wormy food with an offer, it'd have been an inevitable, but bittersweet ending to our friendship.

"Please, let me help you."

"How? Can you bring her back?"

He kneeled beside me but remained in silence.

"So, you can't help me," I replied to his curled lips.

"My girl doesn't like to see you like this." He nodded to Aadab. "She says you're a nice person."

I stared at Aadab, no words coming from my mouth. Even air barely came out. She stared at us with a frown, eyebrows wilted in sadness.

"Your friend here, she was obsolete." Mohammed shook his head and raised his hand when he noticed I was about to protest. "Her software didn't have pending updates. The casinos never wanted to buy another one of her... kind." I could see he had the word "model" on his lips. "So she was discontinued. I tried to argue about her kind's usefulness, that dealers that fully resembled humans were better employees, but I was outnumbered. So, the future reeled forward with all the MGS laws... and a new line of dealer androids came into production. Solar-powered, prime biograft, biodegradable parts. Anyway, it's possible to reboot Lyria."

"What? Why didn't you say—"

I shut my lips tight. The lines around Mohammed's mouth and mustache already gave a grim answer. "Restart her with a new system. She wouldn't remember her past, her work on the casinos, her name... you. New databases, new life. Rebooted and with a new patch, she could live indefinitely."

Mohammed's gaze became lost again as he looked out to Solartop's terrace. For a moment, he seemed to have shut down like Lyria.

"I'm insensitive at times," he finally said. "I apologize for my behavior previously. My daughter lives alone with me, and I'm drowned in work most of the time. Aadab doesn't have friends in school. She feels she doesn't belong there. Lyria's kind, it plays, it talks, it behaves a lot like us, it makes people happy. From what I've seen of your interaction with... her, I can say she can really be a friend. So—"

"Stop!" I stood, legs trembling. "You won't convince me to sell her. I know you want to help, but that's not how you solve a problem. And she's not an 'it'."

I set out to the terrace. I needed some fresh air before that place and that man stifled all life out of me.

Grieving the loss of friends wasn't like grieving the loss of parents. Aunt Monica was a mother to me, so I knew by the rules of life itself that she was supposed to depart before me. When she died, I was devastated, but it didn't feel unnatural. A friend, on the other hand, wasn't supposed to go so suddenly. You were supposed to tread through life's paths together until the very end. And even though my friend had been warning me about her impending demise for a long time, I had always hoped life would find a way. It always did, people said.

It didn't find one for us, though.

The wind of Sundyal brushed on my face, fluttering the little hearts on Aunt Monica's dress. Some people were too annoyed by my presence and left the terrace. Part of the chit-chat that persisted around me was about the girl in the frazzled dress and the decayed android.

On the streets below, a rickshaw jangled. Distant laughter roared across the dronelights, coming from the casinos. The *teddy bears* around Solartop all reflected the ruddy colors of the pillar, from which the rays ran stronger once they protruded out of the building's roof.

That was home for me. But how can you belong somewhere? Belonging presupposes you are like a puzzle piece. If you don't belong, you have to squeeze and smash yourself until you fit. That was what I had been trying to do my whole life, what Aunt Monica had died attempting but never fully achieved.

I wiped a tear from my cheek and straightened my glasses.

"Ma'am, your friend is waiting for you." The smooth-faced waiter emerged beside me.

"She will be waiting forever. She has shut down."

"No, ma'am. That one." The waiter pointed back to the door onto the terrace. Aadab was there, hands knitted together. I gestured for her to come over. I didn't want to see anyone, but the girl's face brought me some kind of comfort.

Aadab ambled toward me.

"Sorry for Dad," she said, her right hand pressing against her left thumb. She promptly turned away to leave.

"Wait."

Aadab stopped and turned back.

"Lyria liked you. She never allowed anyone to touch her hair without permission. I think it was in her... algorithms." I flinched, disapproving of my own technical choice of words, but it didn't feel wrong this time. There was no point in humanizing Lyria. She meant a lot to me, definitions apart.

"I like her." Aadab nodded.

"You *liked* her."

"Dad says she can still be revived."

"I suppose." I patted Aadab's head, grabbed her hand, and took her back inside. Eyes fell upon me. The screaming girl in the frayed dress had come back, better stay silent.

"I was searching for you, Aadab!" Mohammed crouched down and held Aadab firmly between his hands, the red glow of Solartop's pillar falling over their faces. "I told you to wait for me at the table while I was in the restroom." He looked up at me. "Thank you for bringing her back."

The soft violin of the background music had now given way to a gentle guitar paired with a sweet male voice. It contrasted with the hardness of the restaurant, the sturdy woman in the frames, and the tapestry, the one who led an upheaval, a revolution.

Mohammed stood, straightening his tweed.

"Just keep her name, okay?" I said to him.

He raised his eyebrows in surprise. "Aadab wouldn't let me change it." Still hesitant, he fiddled inside his pocket and handed a specoin card to me. I took it. For the first time in a long while, I didn't feel that anticipation of hollowness.

Aadab pulled my hands and stretched her neck out toward me. I squatted. She kissed my cheek and transformed the tight lines around my mouth into the hint of a smile.

I couldn't be hollow.

The Algae on Wheels dinged. Its thrusters ceased. People strode along Caravana Street, from work to home, to casinos, to clubs, their lives all sorted out already, synchronized, cogs that always belonged.

"It's the best algaewich of Sundyal!" Roberto proclaimed.

"Change these catchphrases, Roberto." I smiled.

"Oh, you! Welcome back." He twirled a slice of bread in his hand and placed it into the grill plate. The algae came next, hissing. "Standard?"

"With printed cheese and a few pieces of carrot. Just a few."

"Right away!" He curled his thumb above his pad. The hologram with the price popped up. "Well, algaewich with cheese and carrot is going to cost seven specoins at this time. Where's your advisor friend?"

"Being someone else's friend." I stared into Roberto's eyes. I didn't want to look around and not see Lyria there. I pulled my specoin card from my pocket and gave it to Roberto. He slid it above his pad and resumed the preparation of my lunch.

A couple of minutes later, my algaewich was ready and tasting so much more delicious than some weird carrot stuff.

I strolled along Caravana Street, mingling with the cogs. Not so far away, Solartop's red beam stitched us all into one.

"Janet!"

I looked behind me. Aadab sprinted in my direction, arms wide open. I crouched down and caught her when she jumped up. We chuckled together.

"We're going to see birds and foxes and fountains in Olivia Park," she said. "Wanna join us?"

"It would be a pleasure."

Aadab grabbed my hand.

"And Dad wants to talk to you about some kind of programming training."

"Is he—where—?"

I scanned around for Mohammed, but I only saw a woman with unwrinkled black skin, unflawed curly hair, and glinting eyes not unlike those of Aadab. She wore foldable solar cells from her shoulders to her wrists. Her chest was flat and rendered with little white circles all around.

No, not circles. Hearts.

The woman approached and extended a hand to me.

"Hi, I'm Lyria."

WHEN IT'S TIME TO HARVEST

This is the second story set in the Rioverse, and it broaches a theme very close to my heart: old age. You'll find old characters in many of my stories, both in and out of this collection. I find science fiction and fantasy in general lack elderly characters in main roles who are just common people and not some trope of wisdom, power, and guidance to young, virile protagonists. It's a reflection of most societies, unfortunately. Both in fiction and in real life, the importance of elder people is often diminished, and they're easily turned into invisible figures that are only there to support all that's young and new.

Though intentionally not clear, this story is set further in the future than "Eight Steps to Steal a Yacht and Build a Hospital" and "The River That Passed Through My Life." One of its last paragraphs says, "Later, when the boat leaves the ever-receding floodstreet waters…" That's the only hint we have that the water levels are actually receding, not rising (or stable) anymore. It's a subtle and hopeful message about the Rioverse, showing that at some point in the future, the tide will turn and the world will heal, even if only to a certain degree.

This message is also present in the way the farm works. In "Eight Steps to Steal a Yacht and Build a Hospital," the co-op has a constant preoccupation with safety and resources. In "When It's Time to Harvest," those are already secondary matters, showing the evolution and adaptation of Rio's society after a massive climate catastrophe. In the first story, people are fighting to feed others, but in this one people are already fed. Finally, an old couple can rest and write books.

· · · ● · ● · · · ·

I say Torre Verde Vertical Farm is our marriage. It's a metaphor, of course. Juvenal says it's nothing like that. I rebuke, saying the farm has been our home for the past 40 years, and it's where we met for the first time and plucked our first lettuces from a growth gutter to make a salad for dinner. Juvenal insists that the farm—our farm—is just the means to an end, a collection of processes to feed a community of 300,000 souls. To which I reply that our marriage is also a means to an end, and the end is love. Our discussion usually ends when he says I suffer from GMTFS (Getting Metaphors Too Far Syndrome).

But, oh boy. Lately, I truly fear that instead of our marriage, Torre Verde might be our divorce.

Juvenal wants to retire. I want too, only not now. I'm 78, he's 79, so he has a point.

"We're turnips far too ripe in here, Nádia." He sometimes utters a silly metaphor to provoke me—and make me laugh. (Sometimes we're potatoes, and when he's in a bad mood, we're garlic). His voice didn't change so much since he was a 40-year-old black man with a degree in agricultural engineering and a bunch of friends with not enough food. Both of us didn't change much, actually. We're the same farmers we were then, eager to help the Tijuca community and happy to share the knowledge with other vertical farms around Rio de Janeiro. We share a set of completely human aches—backs and knees mostly—and have a vexatious tendency to forget new names and doze off when we're too still. Okay, maybe we did change a bit. But our farm—our marriage—is still far from being a self-sustainable miracle for Juve to think about retirement.

The pen slips from my hand onto my lap. Again. No textbook writing when you stray yourself in thoughts about metaphors and retirement. I sigh and close the manuscript, a tan, bulky notebook, one of many Juvenal found in our building's cellar in a time when the water level was half a meter lower. He says I befuddle him with my simultaneous love for hi-tech farming techniques and wrinkled, old-fashioned notebooks. I ask why he's calling himself a notebook. He walks away grunting, but I'm his wife for a long time to recognize a peal of muffled laughter.

I put the book on the night table beside my chair and touch my watch to call four pollinators. After a few seconds, they buzz down from the corridor's window. I stand and try to ignore the strain on my back, extending my palm up. The bees land on them, equidistant from one another. My nose isn't the same as it was back in my green days, but I can still feel the slight scent of strawberries and rosemary sodden in the bees.

I insert the four of them into a recharging station and type an ID and a location into it.

"Kids, go fetch Juvenal's gift," I whisper, typing to release them. They quickly fizz out of the window.

Truth is, I'm sad we're tight in this bind. Juvenal needs rest, we need rest. It's been ten years since we've been looking at Isle of Forever Elderly Society, sited at an island off the coast of Rio de Janeiro. Self-sustaining auto-farms, recycling huts, self-sufficient energy generated through solar arrays and tidal lagoons... I love that place, yeah, but not as much as Juvenal does. For me, it's like pistachio ice cream; for him, it's a pistachio ice cream with chocolate drops and the promise of a flawless life. It's all he wants lately—not the ice cream but the community. It's what he thinks—reasonably—both of us deserve after building and improving Torre Verde to the point of eliminating food scarcity in the Tijuca region.

The bees buzz back through the window, slower this time, bringing my pad, one tiny mini-drone on each vertex of it. I'd left it in the germination room, and they fetched it for me. After seventy, it's fairly sensible to use pollinators to fetch stuff for you. I turn on the pad and check the boat tickets. It's a five-hour boat journey underneath the scorching heat through the watery floodstreets of Rio out into the open sea and toward the Isle of Forever. But it's often worth the time—and Juvenal deserves to spend some time in his dream place after all the fights we've been having lately.

I leave my quarters and pace to the elevator and into the aeroponic level. Juvenal is talking with Julia, our trainee. The first thing that hits me is the pervasive scent of cabbage and chard coming from the growth towers. The second thing is the frown that sprouts across Juvenal's forehead when he makes eye contact with me. He quickly turns back to Julia, childishly avoiding my presence.

"The misters in this sector didn't spray the solution yesterday," Juvenal says, gaze fixed on Julia. He's wearing his usual blue dress shirt and khaki pants. His control pad—which he uses to play games and keep up with all the farm's statuses—hangs from his belt.

"We rarely have issues like that these days," Juvenal says, peeking closely at a tower of cabbages. Some of them are already dry, senescing under the lack of proper mist. "This often means a cascade of issues, Ju."

"I agree," Julia says. She's a 28-year-old agricultural engineer with a quaint and annoying way of quickly learning and solving everything she sets her mind to. She's the best we have. If Torre Verde is our marriage, the wedding vows are Julia. I'd also say she's the glue that keeps the farm intact in a healing crumbly city. (Sorry, GMTFS manifesting itself). I keep looking at both of them with the pad in my hand as if I'm in a waiting room in my own farm—my own *home*. Clearly, Juvenal is dawdling on purpose.

"The harvesting bots ignored this tower," Julia says, "and didn't perform the crop on the scheduled time because the mists didn't spray properly. And if the mists didn't spray properly, most likely nutripacks are missing from this section's nozzles."

I see a glint in Juvenal's eyes when the ceiling changes its lighting config. I'm sure he already connected all the dots in his mind. His sole purpose now is dawdling. I put my hands akimbo to show it's clear I know his strategies.

"And if there are nutripacks missing..." he says.

A flock of pollinators buzzes across the corridor. Somewhere nearby, a harvesting bot is carefully selecting chards, its manipulators whirring softly.

Julia shrugs. "If there are nutripacks missing, then the swap drones didn't replace them correctly, which would make me believe packs are missing in the storage. But there isn't because I checked the system... So..."

Juvenal finally makes eye contact with me.

"I'm sorry..." I sigh, raising both hands. "I grabbed one of the packs and didn't update the system."

"Why would you remove a nutripack from the storage?" Juvenal says, and he knows the answer. I seethe, wanting to storm off and get back to our quarters to delete the damned ticket from the pad.

"I'm writing a chapter about them right now. I needed one for reference." I have no reason to justify my acts inside my farm to my husband/business partner/co-farmer. I only give him an explanation because Julia is there, and if she's our wedding vows, then I want to remain true to them. Damn, GMTFS.

"If you remove a pack from the storage without—"

"I know, right?" I raise a hand before he goes on. If there's one thing my old Juvenal hates is human intervention in automated processes. Exactly what removing a nutripack from the storage without updating the system is. "Can we talk?"

Juvenal nods, conscious I delivered him that pyrrhic victory. Julia beams an awkward smile and moves away. She's been with us for almost five years now, but she's still careful to tread the grounds of our relationship. She can tell us straight to our faces that we did something dumb or wasted some resources by meddling with the wrong part of the farm system. But she never intrudes on her bosses' bitter love. Sometimes I wish she did, though. Young folks are great problem solvers.

When Julia is out of hearing distance, Juvenal kisses the tip of my nose. I kiss his. Yeah, we might be hating each other for the time being, but some rituals die hard. I brush off a tiny leaf from Juvenal's thinning hair. My throat is a bit sore. I grab the pad from my dress pocket and turn it to him.

He puts on his reading glasses.

"It's been two years we don't go..." I say.

He frowns at the pad, and for a while, the only noise is the occasional pollinator buzz and the clockwork spraying of the mists coming from the racks' nozzles.

Juvenal shakes his head.

For the first time in almost 50 years of marriage, he's refusing one of my presents. I've got some violent lurches in my life. When my mother vanished when the water levels rose in Rio; when big corporations were still a thing, and one of them sent private troops to invade our building; when we wasted a whole month of crops with the wrong experimentation. But I have to confess that gift refusal hurts the most. Maybe it's only perspective, or maybe it's because we've been tautening our relationship as never before, and it feels like pulling one's hair. Perhaps it's just because I didn't sleep well. But, oh boy, it hurts.

"I'm sorry, *amor*." He notices how I feel. "Look at me. I'm shriveled, my leg's a mess, and my back seems about to crack any time. Next time I go to the Isle, I want it to be for good."

"We can't leave the farm, Juve," I stutter, knowing that's exactly the source of our quarrel.

"Your use of 'leave' means we can't stop working here," he says, taking off his glasses and folding them into his pocket. A cue he's done talking. "One day, 'can't leave' will just mean we're physically unable to travel."

"We're not fragile cabbage leaves, Juve." I snort.

"We're not sturdy growth racks either." He doesn't find my comment funny, though.

I admit Torre Verde is extremely automated. But Juvenal thinks it's 100% automated. It is not. We still need Julia—she's a manager, an engineer, and a technician. She's the only one, fine. In the past, we had eighty people working full-time on the farm, and now we only need her as an integral part of it. Still, she's a human being, i.e., not fully automated. Apart from her, we occasionally hire and volunteer a few other people to coordinate cargo and distribution in the docks outside and a few security muscles from the community to keep an eye on the building.

And it needs *us*—call us the Founding Couple, whatever. It needs me. I've been writing a highly comprehensive book so that future generations can learn and imitate what we do here, so other farms around Rio, Brazil, and the world can have a detailed manual of how to erect a self-sustainable, quasi-automated farm. It needs Juvenal, too. Between the two of us, he's the one with the mind filled with technical data, processes, model numbers, logs, history, and other stuff that I doubt even our systems have. Of course, lately, he's been telling it all to Julia and typing it all into our data storage. He wants to make a point. Juve loves to make points.

He thinks I don't see it, but he aims to make himself dispensable. He wants to prove to me that the farm doesn't need us anymore, like teenagers using faulty arguments to prove they don't need to live with their parents.

I sigh. I've been drifting too much. The notebook where I'm drafting the book is open on the table before me, and I lost track of time. I set the pen aside and rub my forehead.

Chapter XXII - How the Torre Verde Pollinators Work (Part 2).

My favorite subject, and yet I can't drip a single word onto the page. I inhale the musty air of the hydroponics sector. I'm alone in one of the modules, sitting by a table I use exclusively for writing. The farm has some of these quiet spots I made for myself over the years. It's often in a corner out of the bots' algorithm paths. The occasional buzz of a pollinator and the distant warble of (almost) perfect synchronous working bots are the only sounds nearby. One day, years ago, I thought about how paradise could look like if it existed. I could go either with a solitary beach or a lush mountainside, but in either case, it'd have to have a spot like this one.

I pick up the pen and start writing. The ink's nearly running out.

As seen in the previous chapter, pollinators are equipped with nano-sensors capable of detecting when flowers are ready for pollination. Their tiny eyes and ultra-sensitive manipulators can distinguish the light greenish-yellow hues of anthers readying for pollination [see chapter XXI] and the way petals develop in the flowers. Some of them, those I like to call Queen Bees, are even set up to adjust the humidity and the temperature of an environment through signals sent to the respective floor's central control [see chapter XVI]. This pollinating system is self-sustainable and works with almost no human intervention, the exceptions being

I stop.

It's not self-sustainable while it needs flesh hands! If a lot of bees malfunction at the same time, we'd need to purchase or fabricate new ones. Also, their stations don't come out of thin air like Juvenal would love to think; once in a while, Julia has to cross the floodstreets to get new stations. It's not common, fine, but it happens. In all the flow diagrams of the farm, scattered amidst the blocks and arrows crisscrossing throughout components, there's always the tiny icon of a bald-headed, eyeless stick figure representing a human interaction. And does Juve want me to spend the rest of my life in a beachside dwelling while our farm—our marriage—crumbles, and hunger becomes once again a problem in the community? Yes, he does! And no matter how I outline the details and show him how we're still needed, no matter how much I love that hapless wise man, he still fails to see Torre Verde *is* us.

And here he comes. Peace: disturbed.

"Hey," he says, grunting and pulling the chair across from me on the table. I know he wants to parley, and I know he'll try to muddle it with prior chitchat. It's his way of setting the mood. "The system changed the light uptake for the terraces' cilantro crops to compensate for this week's weather."

"Hmmm..." I don't take my eyes off the notebook. My hands grip tightly the pen as if I'm able to escape from the conversation using it. Juvenal brings into the place his cologne's bergamot fragrance with hints of something else.

"This week has been darker than usual."

"Oh, I know..." I say, nodding, biting my lips, still not

wanting to make eye contact. "A lot darker indeed."

"I'm speaking of the cloudy weather."

"That too." I nod.

Juvenal stretches his head to look at what I'm writing. I turn the notebook so he can read.

"I'm not wearing my reading glasses," he says.

"Pollinators, part two."

"Your favorite." There's a smile on his lips, a faint but tender line, barely leaving the neutral ground. He rubs his index finger lightly on the corner of the page, and the feeble ink smears his skin. "Ink..."

"What about it?" I almost roar.

He shakes his head. "There's a—"

"Make your point, Juvenal. You're always full of points to make. You're almost a scoreboard."

He frowns. "GMTFS."

I bite my lips, but instead of rebuking him, all that comes out of my mouth is a muffled laugh.

"I was just going to ask you why you insist on these old notebooks," Juvenal says. "I gave you a WritePadXS 6.5 last year, and you barely even use it."

"Oh, I love that thing," I say. "But I prefer to write fiction on it. All my reasoning and logic for this book about Torre Verde works better when I'm spilling it out on paper."

"Speaking of which..." Juvenal taps his finger on my notebook. Here comes his point. "Need to read some new story you've been writing."

No, it doesn't. But I'm angry anyway.

"You shouldn't complain if I decide not to use your gift. You refused mine."

His mouth hangs open. Okay, I thought *he* was going to be the one to verge our conversation toward awkwardness. I feel bad for an instant, wanting to prune away my words.

"It's rain and flood season..." he says. Now he's avoiding my gaze. I don't blame him. Perhaps he's just there to chitchat after all, and I'm the one provoking. "You know how tiresome the trip across the floodstreets is. And you want me to go to the Isle during hard weather so I remain tucked inside our cottage. It's almost like—"

"What? That the community is tedious enough to make you never want to come back there and instead stay here forever?"

Juvenal shrugs, and his shoulders slump.

I pinch my lips, fidgeting with the notebook's hinge. "I bought the ticket with the option to change the dates if you wanted to."

"We're talking retirement for ten years, Nádia." He shows me both his palms. They're wrinkled with two arthritis-crooked fingers. I glance down at my hands resting on the table. "Ten years."

"And you think this farm will resist without us? It might endure for a few months, maybe a year, but then? Do you think Julia knows everything about this place?"

"Well, she certainly knows a lot more than I did at her age."

"That's why I'm writing this." I pull the book back to me. "When this is done and we have consistent information about everything we lived here... When I lay down all we created, and you want to easily give away, then we can... retire." The last word feels bulky in my mouth.

"You said this to me before in a kind of vague way, but now I need to ask: Is this a promise? When you finish the book..."

"And publish it..."

"And publish it..." The lines around his cheeks are severe. I think of dehydrated collard greens. "Then we'll retire in the community and leave Julia as a permanent manager of this place?"

I say nothing. A promise is as strong as planting the seeds on a growth rack with the certainty that with proper lighting, the right nutrients, and a rigid schedule, it would develop into a beautiful and fragrant set of purple chives.

"It is," I finally say, dry throat and all.

Juvenal beams a kind of smile I don't see often. It's not the smile of someone who won an argument but of a person finding out flowers don't need to grow on the soil after all. He stands and carefully walks to my side of the table. I raise my head and stretch to kiss his lips. That something else that goes along with his cologne is a kind of sylvan, restful scent, something I'd associate with new families sprouting up in a beachside community. He grips my hand and leaves, still smiling.

I thicken the word "exceptions" in the text. But the ink is gone. I take off a mobile recharging station from my pocket and set it to invoke two bees. I'm going to need a new pen.

Later that night, when Juvenal's already snoring his dreams away in our quarters, I decide the book will need at least two more chapters.

One thing I always wanted and never could get is an oil lamp. No matter how hard I scoured the floodstreets of Rio, I never found a good, old-fashioned oil lamp, something that screamed past and bucolics. The recess and grow lights of the farm are always too businesslike white for my tastes. I ended up writing under candlelight and, later, under pollinator light. Many of them are more like fireflies than bees, emanating adjustable lights from their spiracles that are often used to control the light uptake in some sectors. I arrange them spread across my studio to bathe me in what I call fake lamplight. If anything, inspiration comes easier.

Chapter XXIV - Maximizing Crop Output.

It's 3 AM, and that's all I wrote since 11 PM. The pollinators' constant buzz is almost comforting, disagreeing with my slightly cramped fingers gripping the pen and the disturbing thought that when I made Juve smile, I felt a bit sadder.

Torre Verde is divided into thirty floors and four main sections: processing center and management, aeroponics, aquaponics, and hydroponics. In a practical sense, it's far more than that: there are the fast-turn crops and slow-turn crops floors, autochute systems for waste disposal, germination rooms, greenhouses, hundreds of decontamination airlocks, nurseries, control rooms, storage tanks, distribution centers, management floors, and a lot of other stuff that makes that single building feed an entire community of 300,000 souls. And inside each of those rooms is a set of complex, non-trivial processes and components, each of them deserving a chapter in my book. At least a subsection.

"It's gonna take a while," I tell the room, writing in small letters on the corner of the page. *Idea for 2 or 3 chapters: the human components of the farm.* I've been writing, drafting, sketching diagrams, and making notes. I made a promise to the man I love. No matter how I think the farm needs us, I'll finish this damn book and fulfill that promise.

My watch vibrates with a notification. *Pollinators shortage in 13th floor; sector hydro-B3; rack 2818. Quantity: 3.* I grab the recharging station and configure three of my tiny lamplights to address that issue. But before I can finish it, the white, undeviating lights of the room turn on and blind me for a moment.

An alarm starts to blare.

The last time a level 5 health-related alarm blared in Torre Verde it was after the accident that killed Rogério Assunção. Juvenal and I had been in the passionate/euphoric phase of our relationship, not only between ourselves but between us and the farm, the employees, the resources we gathered from bankrupt companies, the terabytes of information regarding what would become Torre Verde, the boats that came and went day by day carrying tons of growth racks, tanks, rotating beds, computing clusters, bioplastic fences, and everything we needed to erect our "manna tower" in the middle of a Rio severely impacted by the rising of the sea. Rogério was a technician who died electrocuted by a design failure in one of the germination room projects. After that day, we committed ourselves to only proceed with Torre Verde's projects once every employee's safety was ensured.

I boasted to this day, until that alarm sounded off and cut short my writing, that the last serious accident in Torre Verde happened almost forty years ago.

My mouth tastes funny as I walk the faster I can to the elevator and into the hydroponics section of the 14th level. Juvenal is splayed on the floor, surrounded by a puddle of water. A harvesting bot stands inert next to him, a water basin hanging skewed from its manipulators.

"Juve?" I say, but my voice is barely audible even though I already turned off the alarm.

I kneel before him, ignoring the strain on my knees. We're alone. Julia went home at 8 PM. But that's not supposed to be an issue. That's our home, our marriage. We're always safe here, right? Nothing bad ever happens.

"Juve?" I repeat, brushing off the hair from his forehead.

His eyes are open and squinted. He seems to be making an effort to recognize me. At least there's no blood I can see.

"I slipped." Juve manages to mutter, which makes me laugh in relief. "Oh, my waist hurts, sweetie... That bot's not supposed to be here."

But it is. Probably replacing the water of a hydroponic reservoir, somehow forsaking its main algorithm since our current config doesn't allow this kind of maintenance after midnight.

"I'm going to take you to the med room." I lift his head. Something sticky coats my hand.

Oh.

There's the blood.

"Call Julia on the emergency line," I say to my watch. But Juve can't wait. I need to take him to the med room, and all I can think of is how it was I who put that bot there.

"Hello? Nádia?" Julia's voice is a relief that lasts until Juvenal grunts. The spilled water is reddening. *It's supposed to be creating life, not taking it.*

"Juve fell." It's all I can say. Julia hangs up. She understands what's happening.

But I can't wait for her. I set the emergency protocols in my watch and put my mobile recharging station on the wet floor. Making an effort to navigate the exceedingly small station interface, I invoke all Torre Verde's pollinators.

Juve passes out. I whisper his name as if it somehow can wake him. I fear removing my hand from the back of his head. I fear even shifting my fingers one centimeter.

I close my eyes, and all I see are Juvenal's arthritic hands opening before me. *Ten years.*

While the pollinators—*all* of them—gather themselves around my Juve and lift him from the ground by their minuscule legs, the guilt weighs in on me.

Yes, I put that bot on Juve's path. I made him fall.

My thoughts fluster in the same kind of logical processing Julia uses to solve problems. A farm is all about timing. That harvesting bot is only there because something disrupted its schedule. Something like removing a nutripack from the storage, which then cascaded into a set of events that positioned that particular bot in that exact place to exchange a reservoir at the same time Juvenal was probably sleepless and taking a walk. Fate. Doom. Call it whatever you like. Unraveled by me, a bald-headed, eyeless stick figure intruding in the farm's automation. Unfurled by each pollinator, I disrupt the system. With each chapter I decide to add to my never-ending textbook.

As I see my Juve flying away from me, hovering above the racks we built up out of love and necessity, I realize the farm's never going to be the way I want it to be. The farm *is* us. And our future is incognito.

The boat waits at Dock #1, not coincidentally a revitalized version of the one where me, Juvenal and a team of thirty-five farmers arrived so many years ago into a decaying building, heads filled with projects of feeding everybody we could.

"Seven minutes to departure," Julia yells from the dock, wheeling Juve's last luggage.

I'm already aboard the boat, elbows propped on the gunwale. In other decks, cargo autoboats come and go, mere nodes in the food distribution web. Some volunteers help us load crates into the boats, but most docks already function with the cranebots I developed in almost another life.

"I had more stuff than I thought," Juve says, smiling at me. I lift my hand to wave. Under the *brigadeiro* sky, unmarred and unclouded, I can almost catch his happiness. Despite his limp, he has recovered well from the accident, but the crutch will probably be his companion until the end of his days, a reminder of how Torre Verde can't be our marriage.

But neither it is our divorce.

After a few minutes, everything is set up, and Juve joins me on deck, glancing one last time at the tower where we erected our lives. I sense the aerobic aroma of hydroponics, gourds, strawberries, rosemary, and the subtle bergamot of my Juve.

"Will you miss it?" Juve says.

"Not as much as I missed you when the hospital reprinted a couple of your joints." I straighten a tuft of his hair behind his ears and kiss the tip of his nose. My fingernails are still crusted with dirt from the greenhouse harvest I did a few hours before.

"But I'm bringing some of it with me." I show him my nails.

He bursts out laughing. "GMTFS, my love... GMTFS."

Later, when the boat leaves the ever-receding floodstreet waters and sets toward the Isle of Forever Elderly Society, I leave Juve staring at the open sea and withdraw to the boat's cabin.

Two bees bring me my pen.

Prologue - How to know when it's time to harvest.

EVEN THOUGH YOU'RE NO MORE

This is the second and last flash fiction of the collection. Like in "Different Kinds of Defiance," this is set in a post-apocalyptic world, but unlike it, this one is completely inhospitable for humans. "Even Though You're No More" is rather dark at its core with a strange sense of hope lingering in the main character. The android is carrying the last human being in its artificial womb, but if it decides to have this baby, would it be fair to the child? Or would it be having the baby only for its sense of purpose? Is it fair to force a child to be born and raised in a completely hostile environment? The protagonist's final decision bears all those questions (and many others) within it.

We're excavating your species. I've been watching from a ridge for 42 days and nights, sitting with my legs crossed, warming my hands on a bonfire, like when you switched off the heater and lit our fireplace so many centuries ago.

I don't love you anymore, though I do miss and forgive you. I wake up in the middle of the night wondering how the world would be if you were here to clasp tight my synthetic hands, reminding me I existed. How would it be if the ice had not consumed your Earth? Our Earth.

But now the ice has melted. The water covers most of your legacy. I'm here with a tiny piece of it. Your offspring has germinated inside my womb for 25,000 years. A small, chaotic embryo deprived of logic but the harbinger of hope for your species.

My belly is cold without your hands to feel the fetus's warmth. I send impulses through my sensorial system across the millions of fibers surrounding my fabricated womb. I heat it up, trying to simulate the gentle stimuli of your hands. They used to send jolts of electricity to my brain, reorganizing my synapses, making me less procedural.

I'm here now, millennia late. Just a few days ago, your offspring has thawed like the icecap of your planet. A glitch in the womb you developed woke it up, and I was unable to correct it. Nine months from now, your kind will tread upon this world once more. I'm sorry to say our seed's the only one. In my rage, I buried your lessons on insemination and womb-making amid obsolete lines of code deep within me.

You made me into a lover, a mirror of you. But can I be a parent? The answer cannot output its way out of my logic circuits. There are no combinations or associations that lead up to it.

Cranes revolve the soil, and drones reveal the bones of your species, your trinkets, the remainders of the stones you were so fond of. I chose this excavation because it's where we shared our lives.

The pillars of the laboratory where you developed my womb are unveiled.

It was a frightening night with thunder shredding through a snowstorm, but you smiled all along. You brought me comfort. You worked with bloodshot eyes, embedding humanity in me. In our last days together, I begged to be made completely human. You said you would. You lied, and now I forgive you.

The next place I recognize is the cobblestone street where you told me humanity was freezing. You tried to lecture me on the reasons why I shouldn't have this utmost desire to become one of you. But the first thing your kind did with machines like me was to embed us with the senselessness you called love. And love is arithmetic, you have to carry along all the pluses and minuses. You felt the cold; I wanted to feel it. You were going to die; I wanted to lay by your side. I begged you to grant me all of your curses. You had the tools, you had my pleas. Even so, you left me out of death. Now I'm here, watching my species unbury your history.

The drones exhume you. I stand after many days. The embryo warms my ultra-sensitive womb. The future child within it is all I bring from you, but my systems warn me there's something else I have to uncover in my code.

I walk to the excavation. The drones remove the frozen remains of your body. You are in our former bedroom, where I learned how to love, next to the fireplace where we warmed our hands. You had to adjust the heater to make us feel a bit colder, and you said it was to create an opportunity to use that old piece of stonework instead. I didn't understand your logic right away, but it slowly seeped into me as the flames crackled and my sensors detected the temperature of your arms around me.

We cuddled up together that evening for the first time. Your caresses sent electrical impulses along my body. I'd stored the memory in the corners of my mind, but now I pull it back. It was the night you inseminated me, though we only found out some days later. It was because of that, because of what I carried within me, that you betrayed me with life. I remember the frown and the crinkles on your face while you gesticulated and unsnarled your plan. In the end, you said I wasn't going to die with you.

Seething, I walked away from home, from you, the synthetic skin of my hands tearing apart while I carved a path through the snow. My routines sent my awareness of the embryo into nested loops throughout my mind, enshrouding its presence far within me, developing the acceptance I needed, and freezing my womb. Logic warding off the pain.

Now I descend to the excavation site to meet your remains. I hope you can help me, even though I should be there, buried beside you.

All my logic shatters, all the coherence I regained alone in the frigidity of the Earth. My fibers heat up, my chest heaves as if I'm short-wired. I pull the ring from your finger and kiss the ice-crusted metal.

I gave you the ring a few days before our last night together. You'd told me some rings are symbols of commitment. I sought this word in my dictionary, learned all about it in a split second, from its etymology to its use in your society. I liked the word. It was appropriate for our feelings. So I found the ring for you. You shivered, not from cold when I asked you for commitment. I thought we were going to be together until death did us part, but it never will.

I cry, dry of tears. I still love you, after all.

With my hand over my belly, I picture your hand underneath mine, thumbs softly rubbing each other's skin as if we can make this decision together. The embryo is here, minute, a reminder that some things are still snug in this icy world, a message from the past, from you, a sign for the future.

I made up my mind. In the end, it's not about you or me. You would understand. And yes, you made me a parent, but you made me human first—even if incomplete.

"Think of the outcomes." I replay your voice, unwavering and tender. I did it over and over for some years, the only register of you I hadn't shut down. "Some things are not about you or everyone else. They're about what your actions initiate, what consequences your actions propagate."

As I kiss your ring—our ring—once more, the crust melting away, I shut down the nourishment of the embryo.

Hollowness fills my womb and mind.

I can't allow a child to be born on a planet of machines that's barely crawling out of a glaciation, a place not adapted to your bodies anymore, without any glimpses of a future.

My dear, today's even sadder than the day I left you. Your decision was made out of love for me but also for your species. And now, the decision I make is out of love for you and your species.

I'll make sure that the future of this new defrosting world will be full of stories—about you, about us, about your stones and trinkets, about the child that will never be, even though you're no more.

TO REMEMBER THE POISON

When it was a work in progress, I called this novelette "Solarpunk gone wrong." And that's exactly it. Like in "Anticipation of Hollowness," here we're introduced to an apparent utopia. Verdoá is completely isolated from the outside world to the point that it's only an utopia if it's detached from the rest of humanity. Knowledge, for Verdoá's citizens, is both a blessing and a curse. It's a blessing in the sense that they really solved many of humanity's problems and devised a lot of solutions (technical and social) for injustices faced in the past. But it's a curse in the sense that if they learn too much of the world outside, then their very reason for existence crumbles. They work because they're isolated and exclusionary (pretty much like a space station for the rich). It's what happens when you don't include everyone in your plans for the future. That's the danger of the supposed "green/smart cities" some companies and governments aim to build. They never include everyone in their plans and become something for those who already have some degree of power, influence, or wealth.

· · · · • · • · · · ·

The Animal

The old world, that of steel and smoke, left many things behind. Bones, waste, ruins. Tales of abandonment and neglect, stories of things and buildings, not always of people and life. Towns where once plastic reigned alongside iron and overwork, where arms moved to seal a package, not to embrace someone.

Adoniran had heard the stories while drinking cups of mate in his village. He'd seen the videos, read the books of people dreaming to escape. He had the nightmares too. In them, he found himself traipsing at night through a world of endless warehouses. The most terrifying thing of those dreams was that, though he saw hunched shadows huddling to grab packages, he also knew there was no one there. Everything but him seemed dead. And maybe him too.

Now he drove his truck along the dirt roads of the forest, thanking the shadows for being over his head as his five parents used to do every day. Pedra Afiada was one of those legendary towns, a place tucked in the farthest reaches of the forest, where it bordered unknown, uncared lands. He'd never come this far on his missions, and he hoped Pedra Afiada didn't resemble any of his nightmares.

The dirt road ended abruptly, indicating the most distant point his people ever arrived in that direction. The hairs on his neck bristled when he saw the patch of an asphalt road bulging from amidst the trees like a tumor. Even though it was crackly and uneven, completely bent at the mercies of the woods, roads like that always made him shiver. The older folks still called them highways, but the young ones preferred pathways. "Highway" was an ugly term that made him remind of roads indistinctly ripping through forest, river, and people.

He stopped the truck in a clearing so it could catch a bit of sunlight and recharge. He fetched his pad and typed a message to Milton.

I'm afraid, love.

His finger hovered over the *Send* button. At this time, his husband was probably in one of the people assemblies voting, revising, and reporting on lots of the matters that pertained Verdoá. Adoniran decided not to frighten him. Instead, he propped his pad on the truck to take a picture. He trimmed his mustache and smoothed his brown shirt—knitted by Milton. He smiled seconds before the pad clicked. He attached the pic and sent it to his husband.

Arriving. Wish me good tidings.

He was in Pedra Afiada as a forest expander, on a mission to scout for ancient towns and industries that could be reshaped, healed, and transformed into the ways of the forest. As the morubixabas—the elected leaders of Verdoá—said, there was nothing to fear in the remains of the old. Ruins were hopeful places where you could start anew.

The forest became scarcer and the asphalt road smoother,

resembling what it must've looked like many years ago. He started to sweat harder in the absence of shadows—or because he was getting nervous: it was like entering a portal to the scary stories of his childhood.

In less than thirty minutes, Adoniran arrived in Pedra Afiada, where his job was supposed to begin.

Pedra Afiada was less scary than his nightmares would want him to believe. The scents of the forest still wafted through the air—the dampness of the soil, the slightly citric aroma of the pau-rosa trees—but there was a hint of iron in the air as well, the kind that made Adoniran think of screws and nails, of carcasses of old-world vehicles submitted to the forest. And there was also a kind of peace in the air, he admitted, in the way leaves were scattered in the corners of the gigantic warehouses, in the reflection of sun rays on the few remaining windows of the prefab houses, which were all clustered together at the west side. But there was a kind of weight too as if the town's own air was comprised of something heavier than oxygen.

Milton would like to see that place. Not in person, no. Milton wouldn't go that far. If Adoniran was superstitious, Milton was ten times more. He believed ancient spirits roamed those towns, unbeknownst that their shift would never end. Milton thought the warehouses—bulky, surly buildings made of stone—were temples for the gods of oil and plastic and that visiting their sites could bring them back. Adoniran grabbed his pad and took pictures.

I'm here, he texted his husband. He considered attaching one of the pics but gave up. That would only make Milton worry about him. His job was supposed to be quick. Map the place with his pad, describe its main features, take some measures of the buildings, roads, and borders, then, later, write a report of what he deemed to be the reasonable course of action to take. Up to now, all the places he'd analyzed in his journeys—solitary buildings, a small amusement park, a few ancient parking lots—ended up taken over by the forest. A team of rangers would come with trucks to crack the asphalt, plant trees, and even repurpose the buildings into something useful if they were near any villages—farms, greenhouses, dwellings, carbon capture facilities, microclimate compounds, or water capture systems would be built. In two years, it would seem the place always belonged to the forest. As Milton put it, Adoniran's work consisted of inviting the true gods to embrace the ugly places. Adoniran smiled at his husband's words because though he didn't believe in any god, he saw the beauty in his work, in the way the forest slowly spread through the lands, ever-expanding for almost a century. And he was about to extend its branches a little bit further outward.

How's it? His pad pinged with messages from Milton. *Tell me. Is it really ugly? Did you see any spirits? Be quick and take care, querido.*

Adoniran laughed, realizing he was stifling the noise he made as if he really believed in the ghosts. But minutes later, after taking the first official pics of Pedra Afiada's entrance for his team of rangers, he saw the first spirit.

It was only an animal. He was so sure of it that he grabbed his gun and loaded it with three tranquilizer darts. Yet, he shook from head to toe. He was sure he'd seen the silhouette of a person moving behind the corner of a warehouse. Milton's superstitions probably got way into his head.

He tiptoed toward the warehouse in front of him as if

to prove to himself there was nothing wrong in doing that. He gripped tight the gun's handle, his palms sweating, his low back starting to ache. The warehouse's gloomy, gridded windows revealed nothing. They all looked like the black holes representations he'd seen in Verdoá's astronomy books.

Probably a cat. It wasn't rare to find cats roaming about those ancient places. There were rescue, care, and adoption teams in Verdoá, so he should be taking note of that. Identifying the needs of animals was also part of his job.

The front area of the warehouse was comprised of an enormous metal gate, oddly conserved for something so old. Five trucks like his would go through it side by side. He wondered why folks from the past always needed their things big. Beside the main door, there was an access door the size of a person. It was slightly open. He shivered. He wasn't worried about all the things that might've entered the place during all those years but about what things might come out of it. Were there still parts of the past stuck in there? Perhaps the spirits Milton always talked about, begging for the end of their shift?

He stopped, aware of how clumsy he was handling his gun. He tried to straighten it into his hands but realized his anxiety was ramping up quickly. He started his expander missions as a way of dealing with that sensation. He always felt jumpy and on high alert near those ancient places, not only due to the scary stories Vô Abramir told—of people breathing obnoxious air in a jungle of stone buildings, of people drinking mercury in their water, of those having no option but to poison themselves with food that had never touched the soil—but because he also knew how Milton would blame himself—for not praying enough, for not being persuasive enough—if anything happened to Adoniran.

But that place was different. It didn't feel dead as it should, a hopeful place to start anew. On the contrary... It felt like a place that never ended to begin with, so it could never be started anew. It felt like someone was *keeping* it that way as if one could pick sadness over happiness on purpose.

The following things happened in less than ten seconds: shadows emerged on the warehouse's windows; Adoniran noticed tree logs neatly arranged near another building, indicating recent human presence; he felt a blow on his head.

The Gift

There was a lake somewhere in one of the many borders that the forest shared with the drylands, the lost world where one day the green would hopefully touch. It was an unnamed lake. Vô Abramir spoke of it with a grain of salt in his words. He said it was a place *of* peace, but it wasn't a place *in* peace. It was a memorial for the lives lost to the old ways, to smoke, oil, and poison. There was a factory underneath the lake, he said, and bodies, lots of them, at least washed of the grim underneath their fingernails. It was the only lake in all of the forest that hadn't been cleaned and de-polluted by their hands. The only lake where fish didn't swim and weary travelers didn't kneel to wash their faces. When Adoniran asked his grandfather why, the old man stared at nothing and pursed his lips before saying his next words.

"Memory is frail, my child. We need the foul, so we never forget the taste of poison."

Adoniran woke up with the scent of cinnamon tea and the sound of a thousand voices weaving through the air. It was

Exchange & Repair Weekend, when the Gatherers brought fruits and herbs from the farthest reaches of the forest, and the most daring even flashed trinkets of the old world—from coins and cans to cables and candles. People gathered in the main plazas of Verdoá with the morubixabas to celebrate and exchange whatever they wanted. He needed only to ward off that dizziness and stand up. He'd grab his cart, fill it with all the things he didn't have a use for anymore, and go to the fair to see what he could get. Whatever was left at the end of the day, he'd throw into the recycler trucks that roamed around Verdoá day and night. He and Milton would get to bed early that day—after a soup of vegetables, most likely, or a snack of roasted eggplants—as all those who didn't work as Gatherers got together the next day for the maintenance of solar panels, water purification systems, growth racks, and carbon capture devices.

"Milton...?" he whispered. His tongue was dry, the back of his head pulsating. He opened his eyes. It was still dark.

"My name is Cava." A voice said beside him. Hoarse, with an accent he'd never heard before. "I'm to take care of you for now."

Adoniran startled and sat quickly on the bed. When he understood his nose had mistaken dust and iron for cinnamon, he remembered everything about Pedra Afiada. He was inside his nightmare, in an adapted room in what was supposed to be a pallet. The voices around him belonged to other people in other pallets, which were clumsily separated by sheets of plastic or cardboard. He could see dozens of them in the rack at the other side. Each had a lamp hanging from its "ceiling," a small chest, and a mattress. And people, lots of them, sometimes groups of four or five sharing a single pallet. He'd never been (or wanted to be) in a warehouse before, but he'd seen the pictures and videos Vô Abramir showed him. He remembered thousands of workers lining up inside them with boards demanding their rights. Other videos showed the workers toppling the racking system, pretty much like those ones, then rising upon them and shouting against some other people. The worst he remembered involved drones buzzing around and shooting the workers, bathing the pallets and packages in red. Vô Abramir had told him it had happened a couple of years before Verdoá was founded as a place of resistance and restoration.

Then there was the boy beside him, a teenager with prominent brown cheeks and curious eyes underneath his curly bangs. He was sitting with his legs crossed in front of the mattress, a transparent device in his hand.

Adoniran patted his clothes for his pad, but it was gone. He shuddered at the thought of Milton freaking out. It would be the first time he'd gone missing in one of his jobs.

"Cava, right?" He dared to say. "What... is this place?" The boy smelled of what Adoniran thought as artificialness. It was a scent he associated with the circuitry used to fabricate electronics in the forest, with the components that the Gatherers brought into the workshops to include in their continuous recycling systems. He recalled poetry some folks wrote on the walls of the workshops as cautionary tales about the old ways.

Mass produce
Amass wealth
A mass of poison
Then, go to the mass
And pray for the masses

The young man shrugged. "Our home, I think." He extended the device toward Adoniran. It was only bottled water. Like with many things from the old world, Adoniran had seen it in movies and pics, but never a real one. All Verdoá's water came from sources in the forest, and it was never bottled. Instead, it was distributed through a pipeline system underground.

"We didn't know you... came here." Adoniran meant the forest, but he wasn't so sure that place could be considered part of the forest. It was in its borders with the drylands, so it was kind of a grey area. "When did you arrive?"

"Mãe says she came eighteen years ago with the folks. She was pregnant with me."

"Eighteen?" Adoniran widened his eyes, elbowing up and sitting on the mattress. The back of his head still ached, but it was bearable. He'd thought in terms of months, but if what the boy said was true, then those people had been there for almost two decades. How did Verdoá's citizens never hear of them? How did the morubixabas never speak of them in their talks and congregations? "Why did you never come to speak with us?"

"We have other friends."

A thrill ran along Adoniran's spine. His anxiety was manageable for now, mostly due to the calmness in Cava's voice and his openness to answer Adoniran's questions. Every time Adoniran had nightmares about warehouses and the old world, it was way worse than that. He'd often found himself wanting to scream in crowded streets where people could walk through each other; or he woke up time after time after time within clustered dreams, always choking on smoke or trying to breathe with pesticides in his throat; or even being cemented alive in a huge parcel right before being thrown into a suffocating, rust-stinking container.

He rubbed his forehead and took a deep breath. It wasn't the time for a crisis.

"Which friends?"

But the boy's attention quickly drifted away. A trio of forklifts passed in the aisle in front of them, each carrying big cardboard boxes—another thing he'd never seen before but in videos and pics. One of the drivers—a surly-faced man with a braided beard and a suntan on his forehead—waved to Cava, who nodded back at the man.

"What are those?" He asked, sipping on the bottled water. It tasted like a mix of salt and iron, but it was better than being thirsty.

"Supplies to our friends."

That word again. *Friends*. It was scary because it revealed the existence of even another group of people Adoniran had never seen. In Verdoá, people knew of the existence of other folks that didn't live in the forest, and he supposed he was before one of them, sitting on their mattresses, sipping their water. The drylanders or the smokefolk was how the morubixabas called them. These were harmless nomadic tribes that didn't want to come into the forest for a myriad of reasons. They were often poor people who still clung to the old ways like addicts. They fed from living animals and scoured the world for oil to fuel their trucks instead of using the generous energy of the sun and wind. Milton feared them, or at least their stories, and believed they talked with ancient spirits of evil and waste. Praying for the old ways to return. But the boy in front of Adoniran didn't look like a bad person—much less evil.

"Do you trade with those... friends?" Adoniran asked.

Cava nodded. "It's how we live. They bring us food."

Adoniran opened his mouth to ask why didn't they eat what the forest had to offer.

"And what do you give them?" he asked instead. He knew warehouses used to be places full of things, most of them useless from the point of view of survival, but still, there might be stuff that interested their friends. However, that place didn't seem to have much in terms of material goods. Whatever it had in the past, it was long gone, and the places where those things were maintained had been replaced by rooms full of people—which Adoniran thought was a fair trade.

"We give our knowledge, our maps, our gifts."

The bearded man was lifted by the forklift. It was then that Adoniran understood he was a gift.

Verdoá was a circulatory system. In its enormous heart, located in the middle of the forest, there lived one million people. From there, fifty-one roads left to smaller communities located throughout the forest, having different levels of technology according to what was most comfortable to their inhabitants. The center was comprised of a grid of two-story buildings and ocas where people lived, all with gardens, farms, and greenhouses on their tops or surrounding them. Photovoltaic poles limned the streets to harness solar energy, while gas lamps bathed Verdoá's night in tinges of orange that made some folks call it Sobra do Sol—leftovers from the sun. The morubixabas liked to boast that almost no surface in the city was useless. Everything was created and planned with the purpose of improving people's lives, environment, and souls, which was the forest.

Around the houses, Verdoá was painted by a net of public libraries, vertical and traditional farms, artistic centers,

Gatherers' camps, hospitals, market plazas, schools, multi-religious spaces, recharging pods for bikes and rickshaws, and vast swathes of public spaces. Crowning it all, the domes of the universities were positioned in the four corners of Verdoá. They were the tallest buildings in the forest, made that way to remember that without education, they would never be who they were.

Each clearing was set with high-efficiency solar panels that were interconnected with Verdoá's power grid. Rising above the trees, one hundred wind turbines spun to capture the drafts that flowed over the forest. Going away from Verdoá's center, sustainable factories, cultured meat farms, and seed banks intermingled with the smaller communities. Every factory and organization never took more than they could give back, never harmed their surroundings, never polluted, and were mostly operated by automated procedures that included automatic recycling routines. Everything—from pads and electronic components to vehicles and industrial equipment—was developed with a purpose, never mass-produced, and only marketed in small scales, never for profit. Nothing that came from the womb of Verdoá bore the expectation to feed a state-level ambition. Verdoá existed and provided. And it was enough.

The truck wobbled through a craggy road. Adoniran's belly seemed to do the same. He was definitely out of the forest, out of all he ever knew and came to love. *Out of the realms where the gods can protect you*, the Milton in his head said with a frightened voice. It was also the first time he was in a truck like that one—seemingly composed of a darkened fusion of metal and plastic that stank like his history classes when he was a young boy.

"I'll show you what gasoline is," his teacher, Mário Freitas, would say, accessing a password-protected cabinet in the back of the classroom. "I'll show you what your great-great-grandfathers loved so much."

He remembered how he laughed at first when he still didn't know all the stories. "It looks like pee, teacher."

"Mãe says we were never welcome." Cava's soft voice woke him up from his remembrances. "She went to Verdoá years ago."

"And why…" Adoniran coughed, and Cava offered him another bottle of water. He gladly accepted it. "And why wasn't she welcome? The forest embraces everyone."

He knew those words were supposed to be true, given how many times he'd heard them since his childhood. The morubixabas, his grandfather, his teachers, his parents, his friends—all spoke them at least once. Yet, he felt something sour on his lips. It wasn't the water.

"Mãe drove a motorcycle to your city deep in the forest. They gave her food and shelter for some days but never let her enter or live there."

"Why?" Adoniran asked that question to himself.

Cava shrugged. Adoniran decided he didn't want to know the answer. Not right now. Outside, the shrubby vegetation looked like residues of the forest desperately trying to find their place. The land was deserted, pockmarked by ruins of the old world—from huge buildings offensive to the eyes, to vast swathes of what looked like junkyards. *A cemetery for dead things that were already dead,* Vô Abramir used to say about those places.

"How many of you are there?" Adoniran asked, taking huge gulps of the water.

"Mãe says we're around 10,000 people living in the 45

family houses."

"Family houses?"

Cava nodded. He was talking about the warehouses. Ten thousand people living in the fringes of the forest for almost two decades, and Adoniran never even glimpsed them, never heard their stories.

"Can I ask you a favor?" Adoniran grabbed Cava's hand. They were cold.

Cava nodded, not a hint of anything in his expression.

"You took my pad. Send a message to my husband telling him everything is fine, please. He worries too much. Everything will be fine, right?"

Cava shrugged. He didn't know, of course. Those people from the warehouse weren't the smokefolk. They weren't the servants of the gods of oil and plastic. There was no such thing. They were just trying to find their place in the world like his ancestors did many years ago.

Cava rummaged inside a backpack and produced Adoniran's pad. Instead of typing a message himself, he gave it to Adoniran.

My love, Adoniran typed. *I'm in a situation, but every-thing is—*

He stopped. Of course, there was no signal. The antennas installed throughout the forest to create the network among Verdoá's many devices didn't work out there. He wasn't only far from home. For all he knew, he was out of the world.

The Poison

Adoniran had never seen a prison, except in videos and books, and the smokefolk nomad camp looked like one. It was huge, surrounded by a grid fence with several guarded gates around it. It was through one of those that the warehouse truck entered, its wheels grinding on a gravel path like chattering teeth.

"You'll meet Amanda," Cava said in his monotonous tone, pointing to a woman tapping her fingers on a pad, probably dealing with something related to that delivery. "She's nice."

"Won't you stay?"

Cava shook his head and nodded toward a line of three trucks.

"I'm going back home with food."

"You—" Adoniran pinched his lips, understanding he wasn't exactly a gift. He was being exchanged for food. He wanted to complain, to scream at Cava that the forest had enough for everyone, that they were welcome, that they should just come to the compounds and vertical farms of Verdoá. But it wasn't true. If he closed his eyes, he could see a morubixaba shaking his head in disapproval. Worse than that, he could see his own Milton frowning and keeping his distance from Cava. *He's influenced by evil spirits.*

Adoniran sighed and patted Cava on the shoulder. He couldn't blame anyone for wanting to eat. Cava hinted at a smile and started walking to the trucks. Then, he stopped and turned to face Adoniran.

"I'm sorry for Mãe's blow on your head. It—" He was truly ashamed.

"It was the only way," Adoniran murmured, nodding, thinking that maybe that blow was his mother's revenge for being neglected in Verdoá eighteen years before.

The nomad camp was filled with trucks, SUVs, cars, motorcycles, and even a couple of water and petrol trucks.

According to a plaque near the entrance, it was called Forestown, perhaps due to its relative proximity to the forest. It was an oppressive view. Adoniran shivered at the thought of all those monsters roiling at the same time. Not only for the noise but for the damage—*evil, the word Milton would use was evil*—it could cause to the atmosphere and to the forest. No wonder some of Verdoá's engineers vouched for a filtering dome around the forest to keep all kinds of pollution out.

Beyond the line of vehicles, the smokefolk's houses were all clustered together. They lived in plastic prefab units and containers, easy to disassemble when they needed to move somewhere else. A practical way of living. All around, their drones buzzed up and down, sometimes stopping a while longer to scan a face. At least those were things Adoniran had seen plenty in Verdoá. They were probably used for a different purpose in Forestown, but at home, drones were employed for dozens of tasks—artificial pollination, statistical analysis, terrain mapping, planting, harvesting...

The smokefolk weren't dirty. Instead, they seemed as clean as anyone in Verdoá. Still, there was a kind of soot to them, in their manners, in the way they talked and moved, in the way they popped a soda can open and cooked meat in a fire pit. In the way they just discarded the things they didn't want in the same bin. If Milton was there, he'd tremble with fear. He'd certainly see them as evil people, ready to take over the good in the world. But Adoniran saw no evil in their eyes. Instead, he saw them as distracted people. There were trees—though very few—and even a poorly maintained garden in the camp, yet they seemed not to consider those as part of their environment. It was as if only they—their lives, friends, families, possessions, and ways—mattered in the scope of all things.

For someone born in Verdoá, it was a concept hard to grasp.

"You must be the one from the seedfolk." Amanda approached him. He bit his lips. He was on his own now, without Cava's quiet protection. "Welcome to Forestown."

Adoniran nodded because there wasn't much else he could do.

"My name is Amanda."

"Adoniran."

"At last." Amanda smiled. She wore a sleeveless white blouse. Her faded jeans shorts paired well with the greyed skull tattooed on her left thigh.

"What?"

"At last we are able to talk with one of you. You're very isolated in your world."

"We have reasons for that," Adoniran said, though he only realized that now that he was thinking of Verdoá from the outside. "Why am I here?"

"I want to talk. I want to make an agreement with you. I want to be friends." She pointed to a leather chair put around what looked like an outdated sound system, from where a tinny, uncomfortable song crooned off. "Please, sit."

He shook his head. Not on leather. He remembered the animations he watched in school: horses, oxen, goats, sheep, and crocodiles slowly shedding their blood as they transformed into chairs, sofas, coats, and belts. It was a grim sight, but it made him despise all that was created that way.

Amanda understood his worry and patted the chair.

"It's not real. Just an imitation created in a factory." She pulled a plastic stool from inside an SUV and set it beside the leather chair. "But you can have this one." At home, most furniture was fabricated with variations of bamboo, rattan, and recycled metal that the Gatherers collected from the stretches of the old world that intersected with the borders of the forest.

Adoniran sat. Forestown reeked of many things. Gasoline and tar; wildfire and dead animals, which came from the food they prepared in grills and ovens near their prefab houses; also rubber, rust, and waste—all mingled in the thick air that seemed to flitter over the camp. He got queasy and gulped hard. At least in Mário Freitas' presentations about gasoline and oil he could just walk out and ask for a few minutes of fresh air.

He just wanted to be back home, curled up in bed with Milton, listening to the melodies of the musicians that took up to Verdoá's plazas. He and his husband would be drinking their mate and murmuring about how good a given song was and how they wanted to learn to play the violin or the cavaquinho. Still, the smokefolk had their own simple things to enjoy. A man drank what looked like beer and smoked a cigarette, smiling to himself with some kind of speaker tied to his left ear. His shirt screamed a belated message. *Save the Planet Now!* Lying on the hood of a truck, a woman giggled with a girl, both pointing up at the shifting clouds in the sky. A warm sight in a brutal place.

Adoniran breathed deeply and decided to speak first.

"You want to invade us."

Amanda shook her head fast, apparently shocked.

"Why would we do that?"

"Because you can." He'd noticed the gun in Amanda's belt, but not only that. Other people carried all types of firearms, things Adoniran had only seen in books. In Verdoá, only tranquilizer guns were fabricated. Even the protectors that constantly guarded the forest never used anything lethal. Nothing with the firepower to kill another being was ever allowed. Adoniran sweated. That thing, that small little thing barely the size of her hand could eradicate a human being in seconds, leaving only memories behind.

Amanda saw him staring, grabbed her gun, and threw it in a suitcase behind her.

"There are hundreds of nomad folks like us. Not all of them are as... polite as we are. We need that for protection."

He didn't know if that was true, but he remembered from history books that protection was a word widely used when people wanted to defend their right to kill those they hated.

"I want to make a proposition," Amanda said, propping her elbows on her knees and staring into Adoniran's eyes. Her breath reeked of greasiness. "The forest is where things happen today. It's where the resources are, both in terms of people, raw materials, and food, but also in techniques, organization, and technology. It's how things should be so the planet works... properly." She waved a finger, finding the word she wanted. "It's the future, I'll never deny that."

She spoke like a Verdoá's morubixaba. Adoniran's lips were dry, but he nodded to show he was listening.

"But you've forgotten some things along the way," she said.

"If we forgot them, that's because they needed to be forgotten."

"You shouldn't pride yourself in forgetting anything."

"What are you talking about?" He was getting impatient. His problem wasn't with Amanda, but with what she represented, with the ideas seeping through those people and that place. With the evil spirits that Milton would see lurking behind every person there, even touching the small girl giggling on the truck's hood. If Adoniran wasn't there against his will, he'd have walked away without listening to a single word of what Amanda had to say.

"What I'm saying is that we are the wealthy ones. Even the folks in the family houses—what we once called warehouses, as you probably know—are wealthy."

Adoniran folded his arms. He was failing to get her point.

"Compared to what's out there..." Amanda gesticulated to the drylands beyond the grids of Forestown. "Extreme poverty and despair. Hunger. Disease. Death abounds everywhere."

Adoniran clenched his teeth. He hated to hear and talk about those things. It was a behavior he got from Milton, but it was also something that perspired in Verdoá itself. The forest was life and health, nature and prosperity. All those things Amanda was talking about belonged to a past that didn't exist anymore but in history classes.

"And you hold the solution in the forest," she said. "You can see me as an envoy. For us, for little Lea up there in that truck's hood, for old James smoking his menthol cigarette and listening to his podcasts... For me, of course... But for poor, young Cava and his Mãe in the family houses. And, most of all, for all the people you're not seeing."

"Yes, yes, yes." Adoniran's throat was sore. His skin crawled with uneasiness. "But what can we do?"

"You should ask that question to your morubixabas." Amanda smiled. "What can we all do for others? We from Forestown bring food and some protection to a lot of people, but it's far from enough. And you, with all your power and resources? What can you do?"

"I'm just a forest expander. You brought the wrong person here."

"*Expander*. Even that word is oppressive. You bring your ways and that's it. You never consider those living underneath the sun, without the protection of trees, right? And when some of us go there, you're always polite and kind, but self-righteous and condescending. And you never let us be anything more than... tourists?"

They gave her food and shelter for some days but never let her enter or live there. Yes, he knew there were public assemblies in Verdoá whenever someone or some group requested asylum or a home. He'd never been interested in them, but Milton had attended some of them. The only thing Adoniran knew—that he *perceived*—was that no outsider ever came to live in Verdoá.

He couldn't blame the morubixabas or anyone for that. When Verdoá was established, it suffered from a lot of incursions from people who wanted to exploit its lands—loggers, miners, private armies, and politicians. People like those encamped in Forestown, with firearms and ideas to enforce their ways to get what they wanted. So Verdoá had to close itself for protection. It was supposed to be temporary. Vô Abramir used to tell Verdoá had a huge army of defense scattered throughout the forest, including watchers who stood guard on treehouses and underneath hills. Verdoá's drones shot from the sky—not only tranquilizer darts but real bullets—, a cloud of metal humming above the copse of trees and seeking invaders. Those conflicts only ended when the drylands became even more sterile and the world outside crumbled, so no group could be organized enough to oppose Verdoá's strength. By then, Verdoá was a solitary entity surrounded by many kilometers of forest, its population living like they always devised: in harmony with the environment.

"You, Adoniran, have a voice," Amanda said. "An important one. Because you live there." She nodded with her chin in the direction of the forest that he left behind and longed for above everything else right now. "We know you can't grow enough to embrace so many people from the outside. That kind of scale would crush your... ways." She lent a kind of hostility to the word. "But we can work together and improve who you are... who we are. And bring some relief to everyone."

"What do you propose?" He was getting really curious about what she had in mind to save the lives of thousands. He doubted anything useful could come out of her soot-tainted ideas. She would probably suggest skyscrapers and gas stations, highways and mass production, industries and growth. Progress. Unreliable and accelerated progress that promised to include everyone but instead forced people into the jails of their own minds, cementing them into a world where they had only the illusion of choice. He'd read all about that. He had the nightmares. He'd seen the rough, dusty ruins of those illusions.

"I'm not that smart to know the way out of this," she said, her voice almost saddened with honesty. "But you have universities in Verdoá. You have people who can... *think*. So what I propose is that you come with me so I can show you something."

Adoniran had grown up with an extreme sense of collective. At school or in the university, he'd learned and put in practice that one should never exclude or exploit anyone. Later, in the religious rites he attended with Milton, he learned to be mindful of everyone's creeds—or absence thereof. He'd never felt the sense of superiority that seemed abundant in history books over any person, animal, or thing in the world. He was sure he was only a part in a whole, a grain of dust in an endless sea of ways of living and caring and nurturing and existing. Yet, his mind never traveled beyond the forest. He realized that for preservation, Verdoá had built an invisible dome around the forest and its communities. In a desperate attempt to survive, Verdoá had excluded.

Amanda was driving through one of the dirt roads that left Forestown. By then, he was growing used to twist his nose to the suffocating stench of gasoline her vehicle puffed out.

"When I say I'm an expander," he told Amanda apologetically, desperately trying to break the clunky humming of the car, "it's not in a bad way. The forest can only be beneficial to these... lands."

Amanda smiled, eyes still on the road. All around, the only thing in sight was the ruins of what he thought had been a powerplant.

"To the eyes of the colonizer, the gifts he brings are always paved in good intentions."

"We're not colonizers!" He abhorred that world. When he was a kid, he used to play a board game with Vô Abramir in which they had to move pieces to defeat a colonial power that was trying to invade the forest. It was fun, and it had been invented so kids could learn what colonization meant.

"But you have to understand that's how we see you." A shadow hung over Amanda's expression. She seemed sterner than before. "When you have and don't share. When we come to you, and you look down at us as inferiors just because we don't share your vision, your ways."

"But your ways..." Adoniran shut his mouth. Whatever came out of it could be seen as an attack. And he didn't want it to sound that way.

There was barely any intersection between the way those people lived and the way that formed the basis of everything Verdoá represented. Talking with Amanda, Adoniran found out they still mass-produced a lot of stuff in factories scattered across the drylands. Firearms, vehicles, clothing, and electronics. Hydroelectrics, thermal, and even nuclear power plants still existed. Out of the forest, the world had crumbled, but there were still cooperatives and organizations lingering on the old ways. Some of them did that exclusively for survival, but the world of profit and exploitation, albeit profoundly changed, still wound through nomad camps like Forestown and permanent cities built on top of the old ones. They relied on oil, cattle, gas, deforestation, labor camps, and a lot of things that would be a hard 'no' to anyone in Verdoá. Still, there was something above anything else: the people. Was it right to not even consider there were people suffering out in the drylands? In an individual level, at least, deep in his heart, Adoniran was certain of the answer. His fear of being there was suddenly replaced with the sensation that Verdoá and its people—*his* people—had forgotten the taste of poison to the point that they were secreting it themselves just by keeping so many out of their plans.

"Our ways aren't ideal," Amanda said after a while as if to conclude her own stream of thoughts. "But how can we share your vision and live your way if we're never included in the only capital in the world with a sustainable solution to the future? Right now, little Lea out there in the camp won't think about planting beets in dead soil. She'll eat real meat. A dead cow, yes. No matter how that makes you uncomfortable."

Adoniran's belly churned. Not because of Amanda's words but of what he was seeing looming before him. Amanda left the dirt road and braked into a landfill that was previously hidden by the hills. As they opened the car's door to leave, Adoniran got dizzy. He retched. He'd never smelled—*breathed*—something so obnoxious and disgusting in his entire life. He leaned against the car and vomited. The first image that came into his head was of the spirits of oil and plastic swirling into his body. Somewhere deep within him, Milton screamed for help. *My husband will die! Someone help us!* He wished that to be true. At least Milton would be there with him to squeeze his hands and whisper words of comfort into his ear. *Everything is going to be all right, querido. We'll exorcise these things from you.*

When he opened his eyes, Amanda was holding a sheaf of mint in front of him.

"Smell it," she said, indifferent to the stench.

He grabbed it as if his life depended on it and breathed in. His heart rate slowed down and the sight of that place started to sink in. He'd avoided landfills even in books and videos after Vô Abramir showed him a video of children picking up trash to eat. He remembered having a panic attack when he watched the video, screaming at his grandpa why he would show him something so nasty. To which his dear grandfather said, "It's a taste of poison for you. Remember you need to taste it once in a while. So you know who you are, where we came from, and where we should never go back to."

And there it was, in front of him: the forgotten past that Verdoá had conquered through the ages. That which wasn't supposed to exist anymore. It was as if he was traveling back in time.

"Why did you bring me here?" He almost mouthed the words to Amanda, though he believed that Vô Abramir would've done the same had he known about the landfill.

"It's called Campo dos Helicópteros," she said. Helicopter Field. That didn't make sense until she explained. "When the word went to shit, many helicopters overflew this area for years. And not one of them gave a damn about the people living here. So someone came up with that ironic name."

The trash went as far as the eye could see. At some points, mounds of trash piled up, crowned by flocks of vultures. A road crossed through the landfill, neatly preserved by the people who lived there, a strip of cleanliness among the chaotic waste. What hurt the most were the children. They were bent or kneeled on the trash, rummaging with their little hands for something. *To eat, to keep, to bring as a gift for a parent*. In other areas, people with pointy sticks, magnets, and carts collected what they could.

"What is this place exactly?"

"The main dumping ground for the big cities still existing in the country. Every day, from ten to twenty trucks, come here to... replenish the landfill."

"And why don't these folks go away?"

Amanda shrugged. "We don't have answers to many things, my friend. That's why I want your help. Verdoá's help. We know that at some point, you had solutions, and we didn't. We want you to share it. That's all. We want to be one."

The fact that those words came from an outsider hurt. It wasn't the one who doesn't have it who should beg, it was the one who has it that should offer.

"I don't want to be here," Adoniran said.

"We're not staying. I'm here to pick up a delivery."

An old lady in a wheelchair came down the road, a smile on her face. Adoniran wondered how it fit there. Her hair was thinning, her brown cheeks tinted with the clearer lines of past scars. She wore a checkered blue dress, clean, not a wrinkle on it. She brought a bag to her lap.

"Glad to see you, Dona Mariana," Amanda said, kneeling before the old lady and kissing her left hand. It shivered slightly. "This is the friend I told you about. He's going to help us change the world."

Dona Mariana raised her chin and threw a suspicious glare at Adoniran. He licked his lips. His stomach crunched, so he gave another whiff at the sheaf of mint.

"Here's the scarf for Little Lea," Dona Mariana said. Her voice was rough and patchy, and he wondered if that place had something to do with it. "How is she?"

"She's fine." Amanda smiled and kissed Dona Mariana's hand again. "Recovering from a cold. You sure you don't want to come to the camp?"

"No, my child." Dona Mariana waved her other hand. "I have people to teach around here. Each day there's more coming from up north, and they need to learn how to eat, what to eat, and how to be part of our community. Things aren't so good up there, and it's worsening. In the coasts, things are even worse with the recent tidal waves that washed the shore."

Adoniran widened his eyes. He had no idea what she was talking about. But he could easily figure it out and it frightened him. Verdoá wasn't that different from the 1% elite of the old world. Vô Abramir talked a lot about them, and he'd learned it in school as well. People with so many resources and power that some of them could barely be considered as part of the human experience.

Amanda picked up the scarf from Dona Mariana's hand. It'd been hand-stitched in fractals of little suns and moons.

"Thanks," Amanda said. "We have food and other things in my car."

Adoniran was relieved when they left back to the camp

twenty minutes later. He hadn't exchanged a word with Dona Mariana.

That night, he had the nightmares. Only they were different this time. He wasn't hurtling through darkened warehouses to find out shadows that never ended their shift. This time, Vô Abramir came to him at night as a very old man, bones protruding from his lanky body. He came begging for food. When he reached for his grandfather's hands to hold them tight, the old man vanished in thin air. Milton came too, not skinny, but lost, sick, his face pockmarked by red pustules, his eyes swollen and shedding tears. Amorphous spirits swooshed and curled all around him, dripping black goo from their ectoplasmic bodies. When he tried to reach Milton, he saw himself surrounded by giant morubixabas, all thumping their feet on the ground. Everything shook, but not one of them heard his pleas for help.

"I want to go back to Campo dos Helicópteros." It was the first thing he told Amanda as he woke up. She couldn't hide the look of surprise on her face. In silence, she drove him back to the landfill.

"I want a scarf," Adoniran told Dona Mariana, as she approached him with a frown. "For when I get back here."

The hammock's sway was pleasant at the mercy of the cool wind that blew through the forest. That annoyed Adoniran.

"What's the matter?" Milton asked. They were lying enmeshed on the hammock, their legs crossed with each other, arms interlocked to ease the longing from the five days Adoniran was away. "Since you came back you're not the same."

He wasn't. He knew that. He caressed Milton's head and spent a long time in silence. He would never be the same.

"Did a pregnant woman come to Verdoá in a motorcycle eighteen years ago?" he asked, finally. Milton didn't participate in all the assemblies, but he had far better knowledge of them and their results than Adoniran.

Milton frowned. "So many people tried to come here. I'm not sure if—" He cut his words and nodded. "Oh, no, I remember her. Yes. She... offended the forest."

"Why do you think so?"

"I don't, really. The morubixabas said that at the time. I've read about this case. People said her vehicle spread smoke and dirtied the forest. So when the voting was cast, she wasn't approved. With that behavior she... She posed a risk to Verdoá's integrity. So she was sent back with a load of goods and food."

Adoniran had nothing to say about those words. He barely believed them. Worse, he thought he wouldn't mind if he'd heard them weeks ago. Verdoá was secreting the poison. And that had to change.

"Querido," Adoniran said, caressing Milton's cheeks, knowing the next words might hurt him. "I'll work as an ambassador from now on."

"An ambassador? Do you mean—" Milton released himself from Adoniran's embrace and straightened up on the hammock, interrupting the swaying. Adoniran felt relieved. "But we don't do that for more than sixty years."

"But we need to now. We need to be out there. And here too. We have so many things to learn ourselves."

Milton was shocked, but he would get used to it. If Adoniran's plans came to fruition—and he knew it would take a long, long time—then everyone would experience the same discomfort as him. But in the end, the forest would expand. Not outward, but within.

The Scarf

Her great-grandfather Cava had written about that place. Lake Mariana was unlike any other place on the entire planet. It was a place of foulness but also of remembrance. Jenny walked to the lakeshore, knowing even shrubs refused to live alongside it. A scarf tied to a pole swooshed with the wind, little suns, and moons fading on it. Like her parents and their parents before, she took it in her hands and closed her eyes. The gale brought a stench with it, sucking it from the bottom of the lake into her nostrils. She'd come there for it. For the poison. To know how it had been and how it could never be again.

LOOK TO THE SKY, MY LOVE

This story carries a lot of "Brazilian-ness" in it. There's the party, the food, the music. I really like what I achieved with this one, merging loss and hope together in a Solarpunk narrative that's mostly focused on the feelings of the main character. (Plus, it has mechas!) And it's a good story to exemplify how you can have conflict in a story set in a seemingly pleasant world without almost any external conflict. It's a party, people are having fun, dancing, and the world seems perfectly fine. But within the protagonist's mind, everything is a mess.

. . . . . ● . ● . . . .

I know how Solândia's June Party will taste and smell before I arrive—burnt popcorn. It's that charred, ever-so-slightly buttery sensation of being in the right place, but in a time that can never be right again.

Alana died five months ago after a quick, but merciless battle against cystic fibrosis. Yet here I am, at a party, being disrespectful.

A mocking undertone pervades the air as I cross the flag-ornamented arc of the entrance. In every child yelping after winning a plushy sunflower in a fishing game, and in the wafting chaos of *farofa*-coated bio-frankfurters, corn pudding, and love apples. When I dare to feel but a fleeting satisfaction for being back in Solândia, it's quickly gouged out of me by my guilt and held before my eyes, as if saying, "Hey, is that what you're doing here? Being joyful... Aren't you supposed to be mourning?"

It's the first time I'm coming here after she died. We used to come many times a year until the disease grabbed her away. I'm here now because it's that time of the year again, time for her party. Although Solândia's June Party is all year long, for me—as it was for her—June is supposed to be our special moment. It's in the name of the party, yeah. But it's also in the way the wind blows, chillier, drier, carrying hints of spending the evening together, snuggling, and acknowledging half of the year has slipped by fast and ruthlessly, but there's always something to grasp ahead of you.

Perhaps, I'm here to challenge the party, this monstrous, continuous entity looming in the countryside. Because how could there exist a place that gobbles up people across two square kilometers of happiness and laughter and dance and affection? Alana is dead. I've set the canister with her re-somated body on her mother's doorstep myself. The June Party should be in mourning.

I walk across one of the roads that branch through all the party sectors like veins. Many of the places are now foggy in my mind as if I watched a movie about it a long time ago and couldn't recall more than the vague setting. The surroundings bloom, remembrances returning back where they're supposed to be. I realize—recall, *exhume*—that Solândia is the party of our firsts.

First kiss (underneath a moon-bulb sky, a couple dissonantly slipping from the quadrille, our makeup—fake mustaches, goatees, and freckles—smearing each other, straw hats too big for our touching lips).

First time making love (hidden in the vacant booth of the fishing game because Mr. Marques was sick and didn't come).

First time telling each other we would always come together to Solândia, no matter what.

A girl with a straw hat, braided black hair, and a patched dress with sewn flaps stops in front of me, smiling, a heart-shaped pad on her hand casting a pink glow on her painted freckles.

"Ah! It's you," she says, taking a good look at me.

"What is it?" But I know what it is. Love Mail. A tradition of June parties where people need to follow clues to find a secret admirer. "I'm going to pass on this..."

The girl scrunches up her face.

"You don't reject a love letter unread..." She extends her pad to my arm, where my skin blinks with letter icons, notifying me of an incoming message.

"Look..." I say, glancing at my arm.

The girl leaps forward, taps "Accept" on my arm, and skitters away, disappearing in the multitude of people lining up in front of booths to buy candies—crunchy *pé-de-moleque* or nutty *cocada*—and tickets to the games.

The back of my neck emits a haptic nudge. I look at my arm.

<3<3<3 FOLLOW THE LOVE <3<3<3
Under St. John's starlit sky.
I stared deep into your eye.
Find me where the devil meets the saint.
<3<3<3 FOLLOW THE LOVE <3<3<3

A riddle. My finger hovers above "Discard." But I don't tap it. Alana would agree with the courier. Even after we started our relationship, she'd never let me deny it. At June parties, you owe a debt with love letters, even if it's just to say a polite 'no.' Love—be it that jittery shift in your belly or that mammoth depth inside your soul—isn't supposed to be promptly discarded, she'd say.

I sigh, lifting my head and looking to the sea of colored flags and balloons bedecking the party, plucked by the sunset breeze. I have no idea where the riddle points.

I set out to find my secret admirer, guilt gnawing at my chest while I look for clues. The party unfurls around me, droplets of memories beading up here and there. A kiss under a booth, a joke by the road's edge, an eagerness before a rendezvous. *Go back home... You're supposed to be muffling your cries with your pillow.* I clench my teeth to ward off the thought.

Solândia's June Party is the world's largest, extending over an area of two square kilometers. And the only one everlasting, going on for fifteen uninterrupted years and counting. The party boasts the biggest quadrille dance in the world, the tug-of-war with most participants, and the most pompous fake marriages, even more elaborate than real ones.

The road slopes up to a plain field where biogas lampposts cast swatches of green and orange across hundreds of white bamboo tables, booths, and sprout-booths carved into hollowed-out tree trunks, all crowded by visitors. Pockmarking the field, dozens of color-shifting bonfires flank the dance squares where couples boast their joy with *forró* songs, hands clasping together, circles rhythmically shrinking and broadening, fake goatees and fake freckles glistening with sweat. All acting as if death isn't part of the world.

Then, I know I'm going the wrong way. Not because grief is clouding my mind, but because grief is sticky. It wants to stay with you. And it knows if I go along the right path, it might be washed out into a bittersweet memory.

I tap my arm. All love letters have an expiration time. I may let it die by not finding the next clue. Instead, I decide to make a pact, to bargain with my grief and make this deal with the party. If I follow the love mail clues and honor my debt, then it won't be disrespectful to Alana's memory. When it's all sorted out, I can just go back home.

I go back along the road and follow the right path.

Where the devil meets the saint. The Quentão Factory is a barrel-shaped restaurant where waiters prepare the typical warm drink using two liters of wine, half a cup of *cachaça*, sugar, cinnamon, ginger, and water. A chiton-dressed St. John pours a glass of water from a gallon jug while a reddened, grinning man pours a glass of *cachaça*. The place is packed. It's June. There won't be a single spot that isn't swarming with that anticipation of amusement and romance inherent to all June Parties.

An empty guardian mecha silently watches from the corner. Somewhere nearby, a woman sings in a boisterous voice. "Tá me esperando na janela, ai, ai." The dancers echo. "Não sei se vou me segurar."

Alana was already coughing that day. She held her breath

after a fit, a few steps from me, her smile unwavering even then. She sported an eyeliner-drawn mustache and goatee, her hair dyed in red and yellow, puffing out from underneath her straw hat. The *quentão* cup in her hand tilted to the side, the dark red liquid almost spilling.

"Don't look at me like that," she said, mocking me, carefully sipping the drink from the straw. She stopped and inhaled, sucking in the air with difficulty. When she stepped forward, I thought she was falling. I felt my tendons and muscles tauten up to grab her in my arms and prevent her from falling... My teeth grating my lips... The aftertaste of a tumble that never happened.

She was only leaning in to kiss the tip of my nose.

"Let's get some *paçoca* before the dance," she said, breath whiffing out cinnamon and alcohol.

I can't remember the feeling of relief anymore, the dimpling of my cheeks as I smiled back at her and kissed her on her earlobe. The after-scent of a floral perfume—delicately sprayed on each side of her neck—I thought I would never forget. Only the tension remains, as if my muscles never relaxed and never will.

A nudge throbs in my neck. I peek at my arm.

<3<3<3 FOLLOW THE LOVE<3<3<3
Where the ground is smashed.
In June, pleas of love, people gathered.
Find me where sweat and heat converge.
<3<3<3 FOLLOW THE LOVE <3<3<3

I smile, then grimace. Smiling tastes like overcooked corn.

But this clue is obvious. It leads to Solândia's Central Field, the place where the party converges.

The walk to Central Field takes fifteen minutes. This is not the only path leading to the center. Like a web, eleven other roads lead to the Central Field, coming from all seventy-two party entrances.

Photovoltaic cells line up on the soil, whole gardens of them chaotically mingled with more bamboo tables, sprout-booths, and dance squares. Underneath my feet, the patched dirt road and the grass surrounding it reveal the metallic glints of the thermoelectric and kinetic generators that underlay Solândia's soil. The dance harvester—as people like to call it—underneath Solândia's grounds harnesses all the movement from footsteps and dances, and all the heat from bonfires and bodies exuding joy. It not only helps power the communities all around but also provides increased moisture capacity and granular structure to the soil of the vegetable gardens that feed Solândia.

Shining in the middle of the field, St. John's *Fogueirão* casts its gilded glares across the party. That's not something grief can block from me. It never could, maybe because of its glaring light: One tall, vivid fire, yet many symbols. Some people go to Solândia only to see it, to leave offerings to St. John, and pray in gratitude or gloom. And then there are people like Alana and me who went for the warmth on our backs, the kindling crackle of the flames, and the shadows dancing in front of us while we talked about the surrounding communities and how Solândia distributed the energy harvested from dance and movement to five different towns.

It would be her postdoctoral research had she lived. She'd promised herself to make that fire shine brighter for a lot of other communities. She had plans to use artificial intelligence and machine learning to improve the efficiency and management of the generators. Once, during a peculiarly quiet evening around the *Fogueirão*, she'd told me how she wanted to turn the party into a living organism, something that could spread beyond its boundaries and supply energy and comfort throughout other parts of the country using a relay of underground networks. Joy and life bequeathing dignity and solace.

"It's not machine learning," she'd told me, chuckling with an afterthought, pressing her forehead against my shoulder. "It's *party* learning. The party will learn and improve itself."

That day, she had the air of someone overly conscious of one's own fate. After a moment of silence, I'd lowered my head on her shoulder and absorbed the soft thumping of her heart as tears flowed across her body. There wasn't much to be said by then.

I swallow the memories. They taste like cooled *quentão*. And farewells. I've already said my goodbyes to Alana. Once. Briefly. As she asked it to be. A kiss on the lips followed by walking away from her. No more visits in the hospital, no more trying to find her perfume amidst the antiseptic scent of intensive care.

A mecha trumpets nearby, whirring its gearwheels and flexing its supple legs. The sound of accordions, *zabumbas*, and triangles comes out from speakers on its bulky belly. It's all graffitied with the party's motifs—balloons, peanut brittles, *maria-moles*, *canjicas*, bonfires, and stick men and women dressed in bridal gowns and mended jeans. The underside of the mecha's arms is bedecked with colored, diamond-shaped flags in many different sizes. Children play Saci hop under its legs, giggling and tumbling, jumping on one leg. The mecha had been one of the guardians when sabotage was still common among all the groups wanting to take a bite from the party's success. It provided security, monopolized energy production, and controlled the booths sales. Now it's just a retired hunk of metal, a sturdy guardian walking around the bonfire for the children's amusement.

My neck tickles and throbs. I glance at my arm.

<3<3<3 FOLLOW THE LOVE <3<3<3
[[SWEETHEART UNAVAILABLE]] — Too bad
<3<3<3 FOLLOW THE LOVE <3<3<3

Wrong place?

I frown and hit back to check the previous riddle.

Where the ground is smashed.

There are always mechas stomping the grounds around the *Fogueirão*...

In June, pleas of love, people gathered.

The people who pray to the bonfire...

Find me where sweat and heat converge.

I lift my head and stare deeply into the fire. The party converges in the *Fogueirão*, but it's not where people converge. They like to see it and make their prayers, but they don't linger. Although it offers light and warmth, it can't provide exhilaration. So where?

I traipse along on the grounds near the *Fogueirão* as if waddling my way through smog, trying to let the riddle solve itself. A shadow already creeps up on me, wanting to be cast over the Quentão Factory and the moments that regained clarity after I crossed Solândia's arched gate. The more time passes, the more I need to just walk away fast to the safety of my pain.

But I made a pact with my grief.

I sit on a bench, recomposing, hands slightly shivering on my lap. Nearby, children hop around a mecha, frolicking and giggling, still far from needing to bargain with life. Night drains the sky, leaving little space for blue, just a blackened, empty canvas in its place.

"Olá," a little boy stops before me, words glowing on his arm. He has a thin mustache drawn underneath his nose. He hands me a love apple on a stick. Its sickly caramelized scent invades my senses.

"Are you giving it to me?"

He shakes his head. "Not me."

I look around, searching for my secret admirer, expecting to see someone smiling or waving—or for my guilt to say I should be home, mourning. But there's no one. And my guilt says nothing.

"I don't see—"

But the boy has already vanished. I wonder for a split second if my mind's playing tricks. But the love apple is real. As I eat it and surrender to its sweetness, I realize that, like before, I know *where sweat and heat converge*. I was just pretending the riddle was hard so I could flee from the solution. And like before, I can't go back there. Why waste my time over memories that will never become real again? Why bother?

I finish the love apple and force myself to stand up from the bench with the same effort I exert to wake up every morning.

The answer to the riddle is the *Quadrilha da Perpétua*. It's happening every day, every hour, every second, a ceaseless quadrille alternating dancers in synchronized sway in an eternal rotation of dance and music and unrestricted happiness. It's where people go to find friendship and fun, joy and lightness, love and sex. It's the vortex of all things, gobbling down sadness and spewing forth joy.

But there's something else. My heart hammers in my

chest. The Quentão Factory and *Quadrilha da Perpétua* aren't just random places that a secret admirer would think of while elaborating riddles. There are hundreds of different spots around the party that could fit those descriptions. Those particular places are central to me.

It was in Quentão Factory where we had our last drink together.

It was in *Quadrilha da Perpétua* that we shared our first dance.

It can't be a coincidence... but it can. It's only my mind trying to find meaning in some stranger's riddling logic. Those are only places. They're significant to many people and famous to most partygoers. I've set the rest of her on her mother's doorstep. I've signed the documents. There's nothing to look for in Solândia.

Yet, sometimes, the only way forward is to make sure there's no way back. I look at the road from where I came and pretend it doesn't exist. I touch my arm and check the love mail's config.

No bonds last forever! This letter will expire in five minutes.

I shoo the children away from the mecha and climb its legs. The unused head-door grumbles when I open it and enter. I inhale the decade-old hydraulic fluid and neglected cushions.

And when I slip into its control gloves and brogans, it molds perfectly around my arms and legs. It's like it has been made for me.

I run. The mecha's feet trample the road toward the quadrille.

Around the enormous square, sitting before the balloon-laden fence, unpaired people wait for an invitation to be carried into the whirlwind, loners feeding on the temporariness of solitude. It's a trait of high seasons, when lines of couples wind alongside the square, waiting to take their turn, to become part of the rows of dancers and be swallowed by the *arraiá* and the *balancê*.

It was Alana who kneeled before me and invited me to dance with her, braided locks puffing out from her head with tiny colorful clips, a tattered straw hat in her hand. I was only looking around the square, thinking how beautiful the four bonfires in each of its corners were, like protective saints themselves, tricks making the light range from pink to green to orange. I hadn't thought of dancing. But just as you don't reject a love letter unread, you don't refuse an invitation to dance.

While we waited in line, Alana told me how thirty percent of all party-generated energy in *Quadrilha da Perpétua* came from the feet stomping on the ground, all the frisking and rhythm translated into energy and dignity for all the sur-rounding communities. And she told me how it could reach seventy percent if the party itself was able to trim its energy expenditure, and how so many possibilities could come from that. She'd eagerly dive into the details, and I'd eagerly listen until the quadrille devoured us. If only we had the time.

And we danced. How we danced. Left, left, right, right, shuffling, thighs glued together in a *xote* symphony. When the couples moved away in two separate lines facing each other, we stared deep into each other's eyes, already bound. And as the lines marched toward one another and we con-nected again, I pulled her closer and kissed her. If the *Fogueirão* was where it all ended, with the certainty of death looming over us like ghosts creeping out of the flames, then it was in *Quadrilha da Perpétua* where it all started.

I switch off the mecha near the square. People gape and

gather around the guardian, clapping, booing, laughing, and singing in everlasting energy.

I climb out of it, legs frail as I leap to the ground.

"Hey," I call to a love courier standing in a corner and show him my arm. "Can you tell me when this love letter was written?" I need to make sure it's a coincidence and not some past letter from Alana that only today was mapped to my arm. I need to rid it of meanings.

The boy frowns. "Probably today, mixter. I never saw love letters from any other days. It wouldn't make sense because—"

"Just tell me, please."

The boy shrugs and raises his heart-shaped pad near my arm. He peeks at it, gaping and sliding a finger over an icon.

"That's weird..." he says. "These things get smarter day by day. It's like the holo-fish escaping from the fishing game. It's funny. It seems to have been self-generated as soon as it detected your arm. It doesn't... have a date?"

Self-generated? I think of asking who sent it, but the words catch in my throat. No need.

I run, eyes hopping from people in the crowd to my arm, waiting for another link, praying for time like I did during Alana's last weeks. A song blasts from the speakers around the square, which is so large its edges get fuzzy in the bon- fires' glare. Non-piloted mechas gather near the fences, each holding a couple of balloons in their mechanical hands, their feet stomping the field.

Foi numa noite igual a esta
Que tu me deste o coração
O céu estava assim em festa
Pois era noite de São João
My eyes tear up. Yes, it was on a night like this you gave me

your heart.

I look at my arm as soon as it vibrates. It shows an auto-mated message.

<3<3<3 FOLLOW THE LOVE <3<3<3
[You've found each other! Enjoy the love!]
<3<3<3 FOLLOW THE LOVE<3<3<3

Beneath my skin, a soft thumping spreads throughout my arm. The beating of a heart, the tempo of a body crying...

Her way of saying goodbye. No hands interlaced on a bedside smelling of antiseptic certainty. No incessant beeps fading, dance steps coming to an end.

The bonfires around the square all shift to plum-hued flames, Alana's favorite color.

Her way of saying a different kind of hello.

I force my legs to walk confidently to a young woman with braided brown hair underneath a straw hat full of green ribbons. My muscles relax. I extend a hand and invite her to dance. Other people receive messages in their arms and devices. They open up for us, giving us their place in line.

We enter the square, crossing our arms together, waving our hats.

My neck sends a signal, but I don't look at my arm yet.

I just dance.

Olha pro céu, meu amor
Vê como ele está lindo

I look up to the sky. Small balloons stud the blackening night, released by the mechas around the square. The night smells of sweet cake and buttery popcorn.

THE RIVER THAT PASSED THROUGH MY LIFE

This was the first Rioverse story that I wrote. It's the one that has the most worldbuilding explaining what exactly is the Rioverse and how Rio de Janeiro came to be the way it is. It was originally written in English as a 9,000-word short story, then translated to Portuguese and expanded for publication by Dame Blanche, a Brazilian SFF press.

You might be wondering where the Dandelions are in the other Rioverse stories. They're barely (or never) mentioned at all. And that's on purpose. They're still there in "Eight Steps to Steal a Yacht and Build a Hospital" and "When It's Time to Harvest." But they don't matter to most people living in Rio. They're not part of their lives, only ominous white stars in the sky. Unless there's a direct interest or connection to the Dandelions (like Néia, Rebeca, and Aline did), the characters living in this post-climate catastrophe Rio (or anywhere else in the world) treat the Dandelions as we treat penthouses in Manhattan. We know they're there; many of us know they're part of the problem; but they're not really an integral aspect of our lives.

One curiosity about Néia is that this was really the name of one of my teachers in high school, though the real one taught Portuguese, not Math.

· · **·** · **·** · **·** · · **·** ·

Dandelion

Rebeca Soares, the relic huntress Néia is stalking, sings an out-of-tune version of *Foi Um Rio Que Passou Em Minha Vida*. It seems funny with a holographic *roda de samba*, sambists flickering around her with pandeiros and cavacos, their sprightly glimmering feet hovering just above the karaoke stage.

For an instant, Rebeca looks down, and their gazes meet. Néia lowers her head, flinching. Of course, it's nothing. Why would the woman notice the short, black, old lady crouched in a corner with a bartender disemboweled before her? When she looks up again, the woman is again focused on the holographic lyrics that descend from the ceiling, singing about the river that passed through her life.

Néia shifts her attention back to the bartender. It's the neural module. Néia pulls the cartridge from it and squints at the status tag. Dead. The way it is, it's more likely the bot will behave like a guest than a worker serving drinks. Néia presses her thumb on the cartridge and it clicks open.

The song fades out. Pandeiros jingling and thrumming, cavacos crying while the volume gets lower. Rebeca leaps from the stage into a mist of dry ice and an applauding crowd. Rules of karaoke. Doesn't matter how bad you sing, you'll get your share of clapping.

It's Tuesday, and the relic huntress does exactly what she does on Tuesday nights. She sits alone at a table and orders a drink from the flybot that buzzes in the air, inconveniently scanning for people's raised hands. On the window behind the huntress, Néia sees part of the Earth.

Néia tucks back the bartender's cartridge and puts it back up. She bites her lips when her back strains. The bot swivels and proceeds to a halt at the pod station on the other side of the lounge. She'll need to request a new cartridge for this one.

A man starts to sing a rock song she doesn't know. He's even worse than Rebeca—who is now with her gaze distant, drinking what's probably a pineapple cocktail.

It's her cue.

Néia stands. Her knees snap.

She strides to Rebeca, shivering a little here and there, but mostly holding herself together by feigning it's the music's vibration. She jostles through the crowd that raises their arms and sings about partying every day, a bit more comfortable by becoming virtually invisible amidst the people.

"I'm the person you need," Néia says it loud to Rebeca, not even stuttering as she'd thought she would. Her tongue is a bit dry, yes, though it still retains enough of the buttery flavor of beer to keep her rolling.

"What?" Rebeca widens her mouth, tapping something on a pad, scrolling through some kind of activities list. There's a communication headset beside her, switched on and ready to be used. Suddenly Néia feels guilty for interrupting. "Do you need anything?"

Néia breathes deeply and sputters it all out.

"You won't be able to arrive right through Presidente Vargas Avenue. Downtown Rio is a region disputed by 21 gangs, 7 paramilitary groups, and at least 2 self-declared governments. You'll most likely get yourself in trouble. Okay, you have the highest buildings all around, but I bet they're all taken. So you wonder, why not land on Alto da Boa Vista since many of its neighborhoods are intact? Because they're not. The fact that water didn't reach that high doesn't mean it's safe. Your best bet would be Pedra da Gávea. It's 820 meters above the water, and there's a base with scientists and military presence there. Settle there, and I believe you can reach almost anywhere else in southern Rio."

"That's—wow." Rebeca lowers her pad on the table. "You've been watching my channel."

"My name is Néia, though you didn't ask. It's nice to meet you, relic huntress."

Rebeca rubs her forehead and smirks.

"If you've been watching my channel, you know I don't like that title. I'm not some rich gal living adventures off my family's inheritance."

Néia nods. To her, that should be the official description of Rebeca Soares, daughter of the late Ferdinando Soares, who was the most famous heritage salvager of the Dandelions—that's what the 104 stations orbiting the Earth are called.

"And what do you do?" Rebeca asks, sipping from the pineapple drink. She gestures for Néia to sit, but she prefers to stand. She's far from her comfort zone, eager to leave as soon as she gets a job with the relic huntress to be able to visit Aline planetside. Sitting would only make her vulnerable.

"I was a… math teacher." And there goes the plan of lying about her qualifications. "Taught at public schools in Rio then moved to lecture private math classes. Are you from São Paulo, right?"

Rebeca nods. On the stage, the man sings about driving someone crazy, purposely crossing back and forth through the holograms of his made-up band.

"You said you're the person I need. You must've seen the job opportunity on my channel."

"I did." Rebeca Soares intends to make her first trip to Rio to resume her father's glorified work. She needs someone to help her. In the job description, she asks for someone healthy, fit, interested in human heritage and history, capable of understanding at least the basics of: ship maintenance, first aid, diving, self-defense, and a dozen of other require-ments Néia wouldn't struggle to recall. In short, Rebeca Soares needs a sidekick. The pay is good. Enough to visit Aline planetside once every six months.

"So, do you know someone?" Rebeca sips from her drink.

"I can go with you."

"I don't want to be disrespectful, but… how old are you?"

"I'm 63."

"It's a dangerous job." Rebeca's gaze sweeps across her and stops at her eyes. Néia peeks down and finds a spot to scratch on her arm.

"I didn't say I can do the job." Néia smiles, looking back

at Rebeca. "But I hope you know which floodstreets are safe between Pedra da Gávea and the place you want to go. You want to get one of the... Catete Palace's bronze eagles, right?"

"And what does anyone really know about safety?" Rebeca leans on the table, propping her elbows. "I mean, apart from the people living there."

"Do you know when to lay low and turn off your boat? Some neighborhoods have ransackers wanting your electric boats." Néia shrugs, just repeating something Aline had told her. "Are you sure of the dose of the sun-blocking pill you're taking? Diarrhea isn't nice. Do you know where and what to eat? With low-quality water all around it's maybe the most important thing you need to know. And sleep? There are jobs you won't finish in a day and there will be nights you'll want to crash at anyone's comfy hostel. Which, needless to say, is as dangerous as eating spoiled shrimp in the floodcenters."

Rebeca's mouth shapes like an O. She probably doesn't get current Earth dynamics. Her father scavenged relics in a crumbling world, not in a crumbled world. And she doesn't have someone like Aline down there to feed her updates. In a few of her videos, Rebeca almost begged for an Earthly friendship in Rio. As far as Néia knows, she didn't get an answer. Down there, people aren't worried about watching some fancy girl's channel.

"Perhaps I can recruit you to work remotely for me."

"Not remotely." Néia sits. Finally. Her legs are shaky enough, and her back is achy. "I know how to dive and swim if that helps." Oh, yes, she learned it the hard way when floods became recurrent in Bangu, the neighborhood where she lived. If sloshing through the water to save your Pinscher Tintin and wading against floods to get back home both count as diving experience, then she's an expert.

"I'll think about it." Rebeca pinches her lips. "Now, please, leave me alone." She picks up the communication headset and wears it, closing herself to the world.

People applaud the rock singer as he leaps from the stage.

Néia is certain she has flopped.

Néia glides and attaches her magnet glove to the Dandelion's outer hull, so white it reflects Earth from behind her. The cable linking herself with Maintenance Door #4 swirls like an umbilical cord beside her. The window is small, maybe 0.3 square centimeters, but the crack is ugly as hell, going all the way from top to bottom. She moves the Tributylborane tank from her back and aims the nozzle at the crack. The gel spumes out, as white as the painting of the hull. Reminds her of her birthdays when Joel was still alive. Her husband used to prepare cornmeal cakes, spraying whipped cream atop them. He always tried to draw something with it and inevitably applied too much. Then, after realizing he screwed up, he kissed the tip of her nose.

The gel quickly penetrates through the glass's crevice and occupies it, white morphing into deep black as it hardens.

Done. She doesn't like EVA jobs—seriously, who does?—but it has two advantages: it alleviates her back throbbing, and it pays double.

Néia pushes away from the hull, activating the suit's thrusters before the cable distends to its maximum. Always a nice view out here, and one she only sees when she gets one of these jobs. At the far edge of her sight, to the left, the Dandelion curves with encased grooves underneath a vast area of reinforced glass. Farther to the left, a glinting white sphere in the distance, the next Dandelion floats. And even more distant, another one, barely the size of a nail. And if she could circle the Earth, she'd see those white balls like a planet-embracing necklace with 104 beads.

"Call Aline," she asks her helmet. They're about 653 km far from each other for 9 years, but still, they strive to keep in touch every week.

"Calling..." The helmet says with its radio host's voice.

The helmet reconstructs the place where Aline is on Earth based on a full environment scan. The Dandelion's hull disappears, and Néia is brought to the abandoned penthouse where Aline usually is when they talk in headset calls. In front of her, Aline's musty couch lays empty against flaking grey walls. Behind her, two tall buildings frame the Atlantic, though they're blurry, not fully rendered by the helmet.

Aline takes a while to load because the software has to translate all her movements. But she ends up materializing on her couch wearing a sleeveless yellow blouse. Her legs are crossed, and that tender smile is on her sun-blistered face. Her hair is curled from front to back, tied with clips.

"Hi, Tia."

Néia isn't really Aline's aunt, but it always warms her heart when she calls her that. That she still calls her that, even years after Néia accepted the Slot Lottery's prize and went to live in an Earth-orbiting Dandelion.

"Hey, dear."

"You're moving in the air with a cute spacesuit." Aline giggles.

"Working on a broken glass, can you believe? Remember when I talked about how you should repair what you break? Well, you may repair what others break too... If the pay's good."

"I recall you telling me the volume of a sphere depends

only on its radius."

Néia laughs.

"How was your week, Tia? Have you enrolled in physical therapy?"

"You don't need to ask every week, dear."

"You know I'll ask every week. Next week I'll ask you if you bought that new mattress you told you would."

"I will, surely." Néia has promised to take better care of herself but has been neglecting it. Headset jobs are often short, but dozens of them drain too much of her time.

"Anyway, what you're working on these days?" Aline waves and smiles to someone by her right. Not encompassed by the helmet's software, the person is merely a blur with the spacesuit's logo over it.

"Oh, dear, same old, same old. Hopping from job to job. Yesterday I delivered 13 printed pizzas. The other day I repaired a karaoke barman. Today I'm repairing broken windows. Pretty versatile, don't you think? And it has to count as exercise, right?"

Néia hops closer to Aline's avatar.

"Flying girl." Aline laughs. "You're bending sideways now."

"Stop mocking me, you silly girl!" Néia blinks four times and toggles the environment. The penthouse vanishes, and the helmet loads the space outside, with the Dandelion's hull behind them. "Now you're afloat in the middle of nowhere without a suit."

Aline roars a laugh, then looks at the window Néia has just repaired.

"Tributing Boring something, right?"

"Tributylborane. It's pretty useful around here."

Aline looks serious for a moment, then grabs a notebook to write the solution's name. Néia recognizes the fluffy duck on its cover. It's one of the dozens she has left with Aline when she was studying for her entrance exams. The blur-person to whom Aline had waved disappears from the rendering limits.

"We could use that down here," Aline says. "Many buildings have huge crevices on their structures, and there aren't enough people to repair them."

"Speaking of jobs... I received the confirmation hours ago. I got a... different job. Not a headset one." Rebeca had told her they could work together and that she intended to make her father's legacy flourish, so even if Néia proved to be unfeasible for an Earth job, she could use her later in another position when the company grew.

"That's great, Tia! Tell me more." The floating Aline claps.

"It's with a relic huntress. Do you remember Ferdinando Soares?"

Aline remains static. Some young boy laughs somewhere on Aline's side of the connection. Néia hears the buzzing of drones.

Aline speaks, finally, "The entrepreneur who... stole Brazilian heritage and brought them to the Dandelions?"

"Well, not sure if it counts as stealing, but yep. She's his daughter, and wants to resume his work. I'm going with her."

"You... what?" Aline folds her arms.

Néia laughs. "You seem surprised. Hey, it's my way of visiting you. I can't afford other methods. I thought things would be simpler, but life here is expensive."

"Tia... Down here... Things aren't simple either. The floodstreets are dangerous..."

"Oh, don't mind me. I'm more worried about the girl. She grew up on arcologies with all those sumptuous protective glasses and disaster prevention tech. She probably doesn't even know what is to have her place flooded."

"When will you come?" Aline takes a step closer, walking on the vacuum. They're at hug distance from each other. And if they could hug, this time it wouldn't be to break them apart, send one to the skies and the other to watch her hometown disappear. Néia would embrace and seize her and bring her up here.

"Four days from now." Néia smiles and lets her hand hover a few centimeters apart from Aline's shoulder. She hates the shimmering intersection of headset bodies. "Send me a location where we can meet."

Rio

The Boto, Rebeca's self-guided boat, trails across the flood-streets as they leave Pedra da Gávea Central Port behind. Néia is silently proud of knowing the details about the port beforehand and sending Rebeca the coordinates as her first assignment. Thanks to Aline, of course. Most of what she knows of the post-flooded Rio she owes to her former student.

"You're agitated," Néia says, lifting her hat (still the same she used to wear to go to the beach zillions of years ago) to straighten her hairpins (still those with the crystal tips that Joel gave to her as a birthday gift when he was still alive). "Because we left your crew in your shuttle back at the port."

Rebeca nods.

She's on the bow's seat, facing Néia. Her hands are pressed between her thighs, and sweat beads plaster her forehead. Looks like a young girl being taken to the dentist. They've left the peace-inducing vegetation of Tijuca Forest behind. Nature abruptly surrenders to concrete.

"Are you seeing those?" Néia points at the buildings jutting out of the water around them. The shortest ones are rooftops and moss-filled penthouses. The tallest ones are forsaken plant-dominated arcologies. "There could be snipers out there."

"Another reason to bring people who know how to shoot." Rebeca glares at Néia. "We could be ten instead of two."

"Ten is a gang. Two isn't worth anyone's trouble." Those are not her words. They even have an artificial taste on her lips. But she trusts what Aline says.

"And how the hell do you know so much?" Rebeca clenches her teeth, eyes attentive to the broken-glassed buildings around them. "You don't live here." She twists her nose as the wind blows at them, bringing the bogging scent of rain that seems to have stuck to the air since the Atlantic extended its body through the streets.

Néia yanks Rebeca's hat from her backpack and hands it to her, finding a reason not to mention Aline. She's not ashamed of everything she did to get this job and come visit her old-time friend, but she still needs Rebeca's trust. Working for someone like her can provide all sorts of benefits.

"Put on your hat and swallow your sun-blocking pill. You're not sunbathing under a radiation-filtered glass down here." Néia peeks at her wristwatch. "It's 43 °C. Apparent temperature is 50 °C. UV index is 13."

Grunting, Rebeca tucks the hat on her head and fidgets

for the pills in her Dandelion-exclusive backpack. The relic huntress has a lot to learn if she wants to do her dad's work and still survive. But Néia is also playing tough—at least regarding that wretched heat. She's used to hot days. She'd lived in Bangu her entire life before leaving Earth, and even in the Dandelions she avoids the coldest places. (She hates when the climate modules are configured to dry and freezing temperatures as if a boteco in space needs the weather of a Teresópolis farm during the winter.) But that temperature down there is beyond any summer day she recalls, even during those Januaries when she found herself bundled with other people in a packed bus with broken air conditioning.

Néia touches the Boto's control screen and checks the chart. It has been downloaded from her headset. Aline had sent it to her, and it's one folks use themselves around there, filled with annotations of dangerous points, safest flood-streets, working shops (and those suited for looting if you wanted), and essential stuff like the best places to have a good old icy beer. She makes a mental note to grab at least a box on her way back.

The algae-smelling calmness breaks into sewage-stinking noise as they turn into a floodcenter. Aline has talked about them, and Néia had seen many pics and videos: broader floodstreets that attracted lots of people. Easier to get drinking water and to find food and beds. Plus, they're safer than the emptier city zones. According to Aline, floodcenters work as utilitarian micro-cities within the deteriorated big city.

Tented rowboats cross the street with merchants selling beer, barbecue, insect repellents, clean water, and local newspapers. On a dock by the right side, sun-tanned people dance while drones sprinkle water on them. The surviving buildings—the tallest ones—are eaten by time and lack of maintenance, but there are a lot of people on the windows, twiddling with clotheslines, handling delivery drones, watering plants... On top of what had been a rooftop that is now almost at the waterline, five women repair an improvised sewage treatment plant. At least two buildings—that perhaps worked as offices many years ago—are vertical farms and gardens. Their scent of vegetables and greens threatens to kill the floodstreets' reek.

"Hey, pretty ladies," a toothless young man says, his pedal boat touching the Boto. He hands a pamphlet. "I install solar panels, repair broken plumbing, recover flooded apartments, and work with bioremediation. I also paint walls, build walls, take down walls... Whatever you need!"

Néia touches the Boto's control to slow it down.

"Thanks." She smiles and grabs the pamphlet. A pair of delivery drones buzz above their heads. People seem to be fairly stable and settled if compared to the days when the floods became recurrent, and her head turned to the stars. Not even the videos she'd watched showed a place so... permanent? Maybe the Néia from nine years ago wouldn't think of leaving if she knew there would be places like that, communities approaching and gobbling each other for survival.

"There's yerba mate, there's drinking water, there's cold beer!" A salesman in a motorboat yells with a loudspeaker. "There's drinks, there's Coke, there's marijuana!"

"Botafogo, Copacabana, Ipanema Dykes. Bonsucesso, Olaria, Oxóssi Canal. Travel fast and safe with all your family!"

"Headsets, drones, select your pad!" A saleswoman sings. "Not even the Alemão's Shoppers have prices so mad!"

"It seems... alive." Rebeca looks around, her face stricken with surprise and apprehension, eyes hopping from boat to boat, dock to dock. She risks raising her tablet to take pictures but seems afraid of being robbed.

"It is." It must be really odd for a girl like Rebeca. According to Néia's stalking, she'd grown up with her father in São Paulo's wealthiest arcology. She probably hadn't lived with the frenzy of people cramming together in the search for high places while three meters became six, then ten, and winter became summer, and summer a new life-searing season. When the Dandelions ascended from their sites, she must've looked out of her window at the diamond trails with astonishment. But for the people down here, well... Damn those ominous white stars.

"We'll have to turn right here," Néia says, pointing at a tight street where most of the floodcenter's hustle dies abruptly.

"Why? Your chart says the danger level is lower if we just go straight."

"Trust me."

Rebeca sighs, surrendering.

"Did you see our names in the Dandelions newspaper today before we left?" Rebeca says, eyes locked on a group of men manning two barges stowed with crates and gallons of water.

"Didn't have the time. I was installing a cartridge in a barkeeper." The last time she saw her name on a newspaper was to spell it out and make sure she'd really been selected in the Slot Lottery. "What does it say?"

"It's about the... lineage of Ferdinando. The... responsibility of Ferdinando's daughter. They're building a replica of Catete Palace in Dandelion #12 and intend to put the eagle there. Can you believe it?"

"Oh, yeah. Your father was important."

Ferdinando Soares had also been part of Néia's stalking. He started his company still in his thirties with the hyperbolic aim of saving Brazilian heritage from the unavoidable rise of the seas. First, he brought a lot of stuff—relics, artifacts, museum exhibits, books—to inner Brazilian cities, then to the off-sea cities kilometers from the shore. When it was obvious it would all fail with the world's governments, he packed it all into the Dandelions.

"A political man above anything else." Rebeca wipes the sweat on her brow with her blouse's sleeve. She still wants to speak of her father. "Otherwise, how would he convince enough people that he'd lift Christ the Redeemer and bring it to space? It demanded a lot of... willpower. Do I look like the kind of person who can carry a 38-meters statue into space?"

Néia zooms in on the area they're approaching. Catete Palace is near but before that... Aline.

"Do I?" Rebeca raises her eyes from her pad.

"Oh, you want an answer." Néia grins. "Sorry. No, you don't look like the kind of person who would do that. But neither does anything here seem to be in an urge to be carried to the final frontier."

"Don't you think it's important to preserve our heritage?" Rebeca frowns as if there's only one possible answer. "Generations from now, people might forget our culture, our customs, our history..."

"I'm pretty sure those people at the floodcenter won't forget a thing." Néia lowers the boat's speed and touches on the location she wants. It propels toward a rotting dock attached to the window of an apartment building. "I have to stop."

"Why?" Rebeca sits upright, startled, looking up at the building. "There's nothing here."

"You don't want me to pee in the boat."

Rebeca rolls her eyes but helps her tie a rope on the dock. Néia picks up her backpack and checks if everything is there.

"Will you take your backpack to pee?" Rebeca folds her arms.

"Do you think there's soft toilet paper in there?" Néia points at the building.

Rebeca frowns and turns to the Boto's controls, ignoring Néia.

"Your pout suits you well now," Néia says. "Seeming too happy around here might attract unwanted attention. And next time, don't worry about ironing your trousers and your blouse."

"What's wrong with them?" Rebeca stares down at her clothing. Néia would bet they smell like fabric softener. She crouches, wets her hand on a puddle on the Boto's deck, and rubs it on Rebeca's blouse.

"What?" Rebeca leaps back. "What the hell are you doing?"

"Put some more," Néia says. "This blouse is too clean for the standards from around here."

"I don't—"

"I'll be right back." Néia leaps out of the boat. Her worry over Rebeca's expensive backpack and her clean, good-smelling clothes is genuine. She's not comfortable in leaving the girl alone.

Aline said she'd be on the building's 8th floor. Two shaggy-bearded men pass by Néia in the corridor. She throws a timid smile at them only to realize it doesn't fit there. Her feet crunch on littered cans and plastic bags. In a corner, a woman half-hidden behind a dresser eats fried fish from a brown bag. She has an open book beside her on the floor. They exchange looks, but the woman rapidly turns her attention back to the food and the book. Néia has been careful with her choice of clothes—far more than Rebeca—but it still seems off in that place.

It's in 803. Néia knocks, an itching spreading across her chest, tears wanting to form in her eyes. When was the last time she felt this emotive, almost on the verge of crying? Watching a movie in an air-conditioned cinema in the Dandelion? No. Swiping through pics of Joel and Tintin, maybe... She can't recall.

No one comes. Néia knocks again. Harder. The door creaks open.

"Aline?" Her friend would never leave her place open, and it would never be that mess that stinks of wet rats. A table lies toppled on the corner, and it seems to have fallen from the upper floor. There's a wide hole in the ceiling. The bedroom's door is blocked by a pile of bricks, sloppily put there by someone.

"Hey, granny." A man walks along the corridor pulling a wheel bag, a beer bottle in his other hand. "You wanna live in this hellhole? Fine. But talk to the neighborhood's manager first."

Néia forces a smile. "Isn't there anyone living here?"

"I live on this floor for a year and never seen anyone but rats."

When the man hobbles away, Néia enters the apartment and tries to find any sign of Aline. But there isn't even a place to sleep. She tries a headset call, but it returns that the user is unreachable. Well, Aline must've sent her the wrong address.

Not rarely she forgot to double-check her answers on exams, and Néia had told her that was one of the reasons she got bad grades.

Néia closes the door and turns. She yelps.

"Damn! You frightened me!"

Rebeca is in front of her, lips tight, arms straight on her sides without touching her clothes. She'd really rubbed more mud on them.

"What took you so long?" Rebeca says.

"Calm down, karaoke lady," Néia says, going through the corridor and leaving Rebeca behind. "Some things take time."

"Like what?"

"Like number two."

"You told me we should get it done before dusk, and then you take a non-recommended floodstreet to poo. Why it seems you're doing it all in slow-mo? If you want to take a stroll to remember your old home, just tell me."

"Do you think I lived down here?" Néia opens her backpack and sips water from her canteen. Her mouth is dry, more due to the anxiety of thinking about meeting Aline than the heat. "Catete was for the rich, relic huntress. I lived in Bangu. For people like me, this place only became reasonable when the buildings flooded and real state speculation halted."

"Then why can't we just do what we're here to do? You're working for me in case you don't remember."

"Yes, I'm working for you. But have you noticed who is leading this expedition?"

Rebeca remains silent. Yep, she noticed.

"C'mon!" Néia says, looking around for the fire stairs she'd used to go up. "You're crazy. You left your boat down there without anyone guarding it."

"No one will be able to control it without my finger-prints."

Néia laughs scornfully. Rio is full of people who know how to make a boat sail without authentication.

Rebeca stops abruptly and enters one of the apartments.

"Hey, it's not over there!" Néia turns back and follows her, snorting, her back straining from the sudden turn.

That place belongs to someone. That is obvious like each subsequent term in the Fibonacci Sequence is the sum of the preceding two numbers. But it doesn't seem obvious to the relic huntress.

The apartment is merely a room with the bedrooms' doors sealed with wooden planks, probably divided between different families. On the window, three solar panels are turned outside, their cables connected to a drone station made out of bamboo, a one-mouth electrical oven, and a table filled with power outlets. There's an iron, rusty bed in a corner, but with a mattress reasonably preserved.

Rebeca stands in front of a wooden bookcase, ramshackle and mildewed but filled with books. She opens one of them, agape, carefully leafing through the pages.

"They're rare," Rebeca says. "Most of our libraries are digital-only."

Néia rolls her eyes.

"What?" Rebeca says. "I think it's a good idea if we take some of those." Rebeca stares at Néia, puts the book back on the shelf, and selects another one. *Rainha do Ignoto*, hardcover, quite preserved. She blows the dust and sneezes. "I liked this one. I've read when I was a teenager and—"

"You little thief…"

"What?" Rebeca widens her eyes. "What did I do now?"

Néia breathes deeply, delicately takes the book from Rebeca's hand, and puts it back on the shelf. To the member of a family who took public goods to space, what's an open door in a decaying building but an opportunity?

"Do you know the definition of a relic hunter?" Néia says, pulling Rebeca by the elbow.

"I've told you I don't like that—"

Néia yanks her arm, and they leave the apartment.

"In Néia's Dictionary, Definitive Edition, a relic hunter is a rich person that calls a relic any item they'd like to possess, but that belongs to someone else. So, the relic hunter goes there and asks to buy it or exchange it for basic needs like food... Or he just goes there and simply takes it..."

"But those books are not—"

"What were you doing in my flat?" The woman who was eating fish appears in the corridor, not thinking twice before touching the knife on her belt.

"We lost our way," Néia says, trying to offer the most welcoming smile she can. Of everything she'd imagined explaining to Rebeca, saying that stealing was bad wasn't one of them. (As you do with a child that steals a friend's lollipop.) "I'm sorry, ma'am, but my... niece is kind of lost. Let's go!"

She slaps Rebeca's buttocks.

Rebeca stares back angrily at Néia, her lips dry and her face dripping sweat. They walk along the corridor and find the fire stairs. It's curious how the public, the open, and the empty place don't belong to anyone, according to some ways of thinking. How a statue atop a mountain must be rescued in the name of the future and a book on a shelf must be taken far away for the sake of a complete collection. But a woman eating smelly fish is just a part of the past that might be forgotten, a mere detail in the scenery of an abandoned world. Like a former teacher.

"Drink water," Néia says, handing her canteen to Rebeca. "But learn to spare. This water they sell as drinkable tastes like dirt, and your ship's filtered tanks are far. Clean water and humility turn Rio into a city. Wasn't that the slogan of one of our last mayors? I think he wanted to convince people that Rio could still be considered a city."

"Maybe that woman doesn't even read those books," Rebeca says as they go down the stairs and reach the dock's floor. She sips from the water and hands the canteen back to Néia. "We could've at least asked her for some books... Or maybe exchanged them for something..."

"Go back there and tell her you're grabbing three books. Give her some brooches from the Dandelions. Make her a hostage, maybe!"

"Stop!" Rebeca yells, her high-pitched voice echoing through the building. Néia turns back to face her. She's pale, sweating even more than Néia deemed possible for a human being.

"What happened?" She hands the canteen back to Rebeca, who takes long sips from the water.

"It's just that—" Rebeca shakes her head and blinks fast. "I just want you to stop being... sarcastic all the time. It's just that."

Néia nods, frowning.

Grumpy, Rebeca sets the boat to go.

They proceed in silence along the floodstreets of Catete, following Aline's map. Néia wears her headset and tries to contact Aline three more times without telling Rebeca what she's doing. But nothing. Unreachable user. *Aline, my dear, where are you?*

A hot breeze plucks at their faces as they approach the

palace. The stench of sewage heightens all around. In the sky, three dots faintly glint against the blue. Ten times bigger than the usual satellites, the Dandelions are often visible during the day.

The enormous Dandelion skeleton at a vast construction site had been the view from Aline's window for many years. Even shutting the house tight and using earbuds was never enough to mute the overworking bots, the ground-breaking heavy machinery drilling through the surface to open space underground, and the drones buzzing all around the carcass of what would be one of three Brazilian Dandelions. Néia had to learn how to shout math formulas. She'd mapped the bots' algorithm and calculated their quietest moments. She figured out there was a timespan every other day when most of them skittered out of the facility to recharge at an annex building. Sleeping time for them, but a silence gap for Néia to explain first and second-degree functions, arithmetic progression, and probability. Because no matter how the giant star outside Aline's window whitened and swelled, there would never be a place for them inside it. And Aline would still need a good grade on her entrance exams.

But when the bots started to fill the skeleton with its organs—tens of thousands of modules, kilometers of white-painted hull plates—Aline's horizon darkened. And the noise wasn't even the worst by then, but the stench. Of paint, of iron, of burning, of whatever toxic waste they spilled on the soil without worrying about the surrounding communities. At times, she and Aline had to walk away from her home to have classes under a highway or in a long-abandoned park.

"Meu coração tem manias de amor..." Néia sings while they weave across a group of islets, the rooftops of buildings too short to survive. Not too much left for they to reach the Palace. "Amor não é fácil de achar... A marca dos meus desenganos... Ficou, ficou..." She sings to frighten the heat, the anxiety of getting closer to their objective, and the frustration of not finding Aline. She also sings because that silence is kind of despairing, but mainly because she knows Rebeca likes that song and that karaoke is excellent to break the ice—be it in a boteco in space or sweating in a boat.

Rebeca doesn't raise her head from her pad. She annotates something, types fast, and drags texts and images throughout the screen.

"Hey..." Néia touches Rebeca's arm. "I said something back there about making hostages, and you got upset. I'm sorry. I—When I'm too worried and anxious, I get a little bit more sarcastic than usual."

Rebeca faces her with furious lines forming on her brows.

"Okay," Néia says. "A lot more sarcastic."

Rebeca turns to face what remains of the Catete Palace, the buttresses, and the plain surface of the rooftop. She types something on her pad. Of the five eagles that once stood atop it, ready to soar, there's only one now, right in the middle. A leader without followers.

Rebeca clears her throat, still not looking at Néia and without stopping from typing.

"Não posso definir aquele azul..."

Néia extends her hand and puts it in front of Rebeca's mouth like a microphone. Somewhere within her, something becomes lighter.

"Não era do céu... Nem era do mar..." Rebeca goes on.

Néia nods in approval. "Score: seven out of ten."

"My father listened to it when he was cataloging rescued heritage. It stuck." Rebeca's smile is a hint of nostalgia, but she soon gets grave again. "Sorry for yelling at you."

Néia smiles and shakes her head dismissively.

"It stuck to me too. I danced to this in real *rodas de samba*, not that holo-joke." Néia laughs. "And listened to it on my phone when I was home." Her phone had been playing the song on repeat when she made up her mind and accepted the lottery prize. It was Christmas, raining heavily. She was watching the water invading her bedroom and eating *rabanadas* with her legs crossed upon the sofa, rolling down her phone's screen through her 19,312 unread e-mails, sorting out something different than ads for mountain real states, arcologies, and fraudulent companies promising immigration miracles.

"Who is Aline?" Rebeca says, not even raising her eyes from her pad while making annotations.

Néia stiffens. Her belly roils.

When she asked a challenging question to her students, a few of them looked away and pretended they didn't listen. It's what she does now, her nape itching with sweat.

"You filed 70 requests over the years to get her a slot in one of the Dandelions." Rebeca uses her pad to take a picture of the palace. "If you were going to work for me, I had to do some research. As you did with me."

Néia remains in silence, rubbing her lips on each other, staring down at the water sprinkled on her shoes. She has always treated Aline as a personal secret. Not because she has anything to hide about her friendship with the girl who stayed on Earth, but because she knows the mind connections people will make. In the end, it all boils down to the same question she has been asking herself for almost a decade. If her family is dead, and she's so fond of her former student, why the hell would she want to live alone in space?

"It's almost on the water level," Rebeca says. Néia blinks, feeling as if weights have been removed from her shoulders with the change of subject.

Rebeca checks some readouts on her pad. "More people could lend us a hand to put the eagle on the boat."

"We can do it." Though now she isn't sure of anything.

The boat thumps on the moss-strewed parapet of the palace.

They're here. They'll put the eagle on the boat's stern, sail back to Rebeca's ship, and she'd get the best payment of her life. Then, she'd go back to her weather-controlled, purified-air life to eat super-healthy, hydroponics-grown vegetable salad in a dining hall with a view to Earth. Without even visiting Aline.

Rebeca sets up everything they need to bring the eagle into the boat. Lubricant, a couple of harnesses, and an aluminum ramp. It's the first time Néia sees the girl taking the helm of the expedition, but it's unfair. Néia's chest always weighs when someone mentions Aline, and the fact she wasn't at the place she said she would be just makes it hurt a tad more.

"Why the eagles?" Néia speaks to forget Aline, taking a long sip of her canteen. The sun is reaching its highest point. Her watch shows 45 °C. UV index is 15. "They were never so remarkable."

"It was the next item on my father's to-do list." Rebeca hops off the boat and walks toward the eagle, reading something on her pad. Néia follows her. "In the day he died, he... thought he'd soon be cancer-free and ready to come down here to get the eagles."

"Your father..." Néia adjusts the hat on Rebeca's head. "He thought the world had ended, didn't he?"

"Don't you think?"

"Well... I always thought the world would end when people couldn't live on it anymore."

Rebeca frowns and raises a finger, stopping a few meters from the eagle. It's slightly bent to the right. Its feathers are tarnished and dented, and half of its left wing is broken with rust-filled cracks. The floor is scrawled with lines that follow a straight path from the back of the rooftop to where the eagle stands on a slightly elevated battlement.

"This is not bronze." Rebeca swivels to look around, her brows creasing. "This is not the original eagle."

Three masked people climb up from the parapets. Two come from the left, one from the right. A drone rises after them, a flying scorpion with a gun where the sting should be. Néia's back tenses up.

"Don't move," says a teenager whose voice's still thickening. Néia can't decide whether his knife's handle is thinner than his arms. The three of them wear balaclavas and move in slow steps around them, awkwardly rehearsed. Two boys and one girl. The drone is the problem. It buzzes around their heads, encircling them.

"You can take our stuff," Néia says, raising her hands. She elbows Rebeca. "Raise your hands, girl. Have you never been robbed?"

"Two isn't worth anyone's trouble now?" Rebeca says between her teeth. "Our boat is over there." Rebeca indicates the place where they docked.

One of the slimmest robbers, a boy, looks at the drone as if that thing can approve anything.

"We don't want the boat. We want... you." He points to Rebeca. "Come with us."

"Me? Why me?" Rebeca peeks at Néia as if she'll be able to provide an answer as she has been doing up to now. And she knows the answer pretty well but wouldn't say it. Rebeca is the daughter of a famous man and insists on showing her face on silly videos every week. Someone in the floodcenter must've rattled them.

Néia walks closer to Rebeca. The girl is visibly shaking, and sweating, with her lips bleached of color. Tears run down her cheeks. Excellent reaction for someone who intends to brave a flooded city after relics.

"Hey…" Néia says, touching Rebeca's hands. "Everything is going to be fine." She doesn't know anything, but it's what she used to tell Aline when the girl kept getting bad grades and thought she would never succeed in her entrance exams.

The drone flies closer, and the group follows it, closing in on them. One of the boys is so afraid that the knife visibly trembles in his hand.

"We want your… slots," the slim boy says, his eyes panning back and forth from the drone.

Néia snorts without releasing Rebeca's hand. Probably they hadn't thought of the bureaucracy involved in transferring a slot to someone else. It would never work.

The drone swirls and stops in front of Rebeca, its sting gun extending at her.

"Wait." Néia steps forward and stands between Rebeca and the gun, one arm behind so she wouldn't release Rebeca's hand. The scorpion's sting slumps quickly. Néia has one of her hands still up but is more relaxed now that she knows the sum of the three young robbers' ages probably doesn't add up to 63. "If you want to take her with you, then take me too. We're together in this."

"Stay safe, Néia," Rebeca says, voice shaken and seemingly unaware of how inexperienced those guys are. "You don't owe me anything."

"Oh, but you do. If you die, who's going to pay me?"

"Actually, it's all set—"

Néia roars. "Shut up."

The girl swings the knife in front of them. A comical move.

Rebeca recoils and shuts her eyes.

"What?" Néia lets go of Rebeca's hand and folds her arms, facing the armed girl. "You probably don't know how to cut bread with this thing."

The scorpion's sting points at them, then to the back of the palace. They'll take both of them. They took the bait. Well, not exactly bait because Néia has no idea of what she's going to do. But she can't leave the relic huntress on her own. Clearly, she isn't able to survive all by herself. Furthermore, a job is like an equation: if it doesn't have a conclusion, then it isn't useful. And Néia never left a job unfinished before. Won't be the first time.

The last time Néia opened up her eyes to the morning rain in an empty apartment was when her family died in the landslide. Joel had taken Tintin to visit her sister Clara. Néia refused to go. Aline's entrance exams would happen two weeks from that day, and she was still struggling to understand probability. Most of the questions Néia sketched to her on her set of notebooks with cute covers ended up with wrong answers. You had a 60% chance of getting struck by lightning, according to Aline. A 50% chance of winning big in the lottery... So Néia would remain with Aline, day after day, Sundays included, until she got the grip of probability. Clara could wait.

When she received the news about the landslide, all she could think of was how the outcome could've been different. She could've been there with them. When she thought about Clara's carrot cake covered with chocolate syrup, she really considered going, so perhaps 50/50 between going and staying. She'd told Joel to wait a few days, and she would manage to find the time to go with them. A proper family reunion. But her hubby was stubborn, and Clara wanted to cuddle Tintin's white belly. So... Maybe 20/80 between Joel waiting a few days and going right away. And there was Aline, of course, and that was a 0/100 between leaving Aline unprepared for the upcoming exams and writing a new batch of probability exercises.

That day had finished with a cop ushering Néia to an empty apartment building in the area. With the heavy rain's consequences and the floods spreading across the city, it wouldn't be safe to come back home. Neither did she want. She had laid on folded bedsheets on the floor, wanting her eyes to close and never to open again, but they remained open until the morning drizzle patted the windows.

Now, years later, having crossed mesosphere and stratosphere back and forth, all she feels about that day, laid down and looking around another empty apartment with its peeled-off walls and loosened parquet flooring, is the 100% of inevitability.

And the urge to pee.

"I need to go to the bathroom," Néia says it loud, sitting on the oddly comfortable mattress and straightening her back. They arrived exhausted due to the scorching heat, and the masked teenagers brought water and sandwiches for dinner. Rebeca was grumpy the whole night, and they hardly talked. At some point before dawn, someone brought a portable air conditioning system and closed the mildewed shutters to block morning sunlight. But the most baffling of it all are the slices of quality bread and the jug of water they'd put on a nightstand near the door. Certainly to please the girl. Being rich makes you valuable.

"Hey, boys!" Néia calls again. "I don't have your perfect bladders anymore. I need to pee."

Rebeca wakes up and groans, glaring at her.

"This time, it's only number one." Néia shrugs and stands.

"Hey…" Rebeca rubs her reddened eyes. She's been crying again. "Thank you for yesterday."

"I'm just working."

Rebeca nods and straightens to sit on her mattress. Somewhere outside, a child yells some kind of order. Another one laughs.

"Are you feeling better now?" Néia asks, looking around and shrugging. "We're still their hostages."

"I'm better. Back in the Palace—It's just that—" Rebeca hesitates, her gaze lost in her hands, which were propped on her knees. She raises her head and stares at Néia, her eyes inquisitive as if in doubt if she could really keep talking. "Mom was kidnapped once. They asked for the company's money. Dad paid, of course, but I was a child and I heard Mom talking—crying—with Dad, telling him about how the kidnappers took her to a vacant lot and pointed guns at her, wrapped a plastic bag around her head and—I remember being so afraid of plastic bags at the time, can you believe?"

Rebeca giggles and then snorts, probably realizing she said more than intended. Néia remains in silence, giving the space for her to go on. By the way Rebeca inspects her own hands, those are not words she's used to speaking. Maybe one or two friends know about it, perhaps some family, but not many people. At that moment, Néia isn't in the position of an employee anymore, and Rebeca isn't only her boss.

Néia crouches, grunting with a sharp twinge on her back. She stares at Rebeca. That seems to indicate that the girl can go on.

"Dad started talking with me every day for months after the kidnapping. At first, I thought he'd try to comfort me, but he only told me about his routine in the city. How he spent two weeks sleeping in the National Museum to catalog some rare artifacts or how he spent weeks in Rio's historical center looking for what he called 'gigantic little things.' Rare books, paintings, and even storefronts of some shops that had been destroyed like the Colombo Confectionery. Only when I got older that I understood why he did that every day."

Néia nods in understanding.

"He wanted you to know what his job was like," Néia says.

Rebeca nods, blinking fast as if waking up from a trance.

"I'm sorry..." Néia says. It's funny how it was similar to talking to a student full of frustrations, almost a personality career test with someone who's about to study medicine but finds out the magic of engineering. Néia considers asking if Rebeca really wants to be a... heritage collector. If even after seeing how life down there actually is—even after learning that not everything (almost nothing) is like a heroic adventure—she still wants to risk herself through the floodstreets in a quest for the past.

But that's not the time for that question.

"Stay cool because those folks in the Palace were... inexperienced. We'll find a way out of this."

Rebeca pinches her lips and nods.

"You want to pee..." Rebeca says, forcing a smile. She's

calmer now, it seems. It's been many years since Néia last taught classes, but her educator side feels a little bit of that underpaid and ephemeral pride of the Rio de Janeiro teachers.

"Hey, you useless folks!" Néia yells, then murmurs to Rebeca: "Now I'm really going to piss on my pants."

Someone opens the door. A woman holding a submachine gun. She's older than the other kids. She wears t-shirts wrapped around her head that make her look like a clumsy ninja. Rebeca sits on the floor, leaning against the wall, her lips quivering in fear.

"I need to pee," Néia says. "You look more like a leader."

The woman points at the bathroom. It's right on the other side of the bedroom, across a narrow hallway. When Néia enters, the Clumsy Ninja forces the door open.

"You want to watch?" Néia grits her teeth and stares at the leader's covered face.

The woman points to the end of the hallway that leads to the living room.

"You want me to go?"

The Clumsy Ninja assents.

Néia shakes her head.

"You do what you gotta do with my friend. Transfer our slots if you think you can ask her for money, tell her to sing for you... Whatever. I'll wait and go back with her. And, by the way..." Néia unzips and lowers her pants, then sits on the toilet. "Watch me pee if that's what you want."

The Clumsy Ninja gently closes the door.

When Néia gets back to the bedroom, the Clumsy Ninja has already set three stools and taken her place face to face with Rebeca.

Néia takes the remaining seat.

Rebeca licks her lips impatiently, her brushed-out brows creased, pressing her hands between her knees.

The Clumsy Ninja gives them the glasses of water from the nightstand. Néia takes a long sip.

"Perfectly drinkable water..." Néia slowly nods in approval. "Why would you spend it with us? And those sandwiches yesterday... They're better than the Dandelions' printed ones."

She puts the glass on the floor and looks back at the mattresses behind them. The one she slept on is brand new, probably sacked from a supermarket, but Rebeca's is but a tattered piece of trash. Their difference is striking, as if...

Néia's lip flutters. The room crimps around her for an instant, blackening and losing its colors. Her stomach curls. Like when she first heard on the news her street had been flooded. Before getting used to it.

It's not Rebeca who's important to them.

"What happened?" Rebeca elbows Néia and looks back at the head-covered woman. "Are you okay?"

Néia stands. Her armpits itch, her arms feel heavy, and the cold sweat sticks to her skin like a plastered woolen t-shirt worn in the wrong season. She steps toward the woman, which shifts on the stool and straightens her back.

She yanks out the t-shirts around Clumsy Ninja's head.

Aline drops the gun, wiping the tears from her eyelashes like she did when she got a bad grade on one of Néia's mock exams or when the bots working on the Dandelion outside her window grew so loud and chaotic that she cringed into a corner, incapable of understanding anything except that probability was calculated by dividing favorable outcomes by the total number of possible outcomes.

Néia shivers. She walks back and falls sitting on the stool.

Her back strains. Her student, her friend, the one whom she left behind in a drowning Rio, is now a criminal.

"So this is Aline..." Rebeca mutters.

Damn. Everything Néia doesn't need right now is to be caught in this mess in the middle of a job. All her sturdiness and leadership to lead Rebeca across the floodstreets is now vanished behind an emotional old woman who wishes she'd never won the lottery.

"You've pointed a gun at me," Néia says. Firm. Loud. As if accusing a student of lacking respect for a teacher.

"Never at you, Tia. Only at her." Aline indicates Rebeca with her chin. Her mouth contorts in disdain.

"And you used to despise guns..."

"And you were picky about your friends..." Aline glares at Rebeca. "Of all people, one of the Soares."

"What about them?" She can't take her eyes off Aline. Her head riles with thoughts of how they talked over the headset just a few days ago. Aline had a smile on her face. The first thing Néia would do when she met Aline was to give her tight hug, but the first thing Aline did was kidnap her.

"Tell her about the slots, Soares." Aline's cheeks are sunburnt and oily with sweat. "The ones your father held."

Rebeca pinches her lips and avoids both their gazes. A student flinching away from a demanding teacher.

"My father... No. I won't put the blame on a dead man. I've held 100 slots under my family's name. I... bought them."

"You bought?" Néia sputters out. "You could... You have a place for 100 souls, and you just use it as an asset? Who are they for?"

"I intended to... recruit people from planetside... To work on the company, that is. I really have faith in what we can do for future generations." Her way of moving her hands, her choice of words... It's like she's on a stage talking about how to boost a business. The girl scared about kidnapping is nowhere to be seen, and neither is the frightened lady talking about her dad's routine. For an instant, Néia wants to smack her face with a fist.

Néia opens her mouth to speak, but only a sigh comes out. What now? Is she going to be heartbroken because her boss, the fancy daughter of the man who stole away Rio's heritage, has disappointed her by transforming slots into job opportunities?

"I won't try to say that it's fair." The entrepreneur vanishes from Rebeca, and all that remains is the ashamed girl. "I knew what I was doing all along."

"Both of you." Néia stands and walks to the door, putting pressure on her frail legs. "Do whatever kidnapping chitchat you want to do. I'm out."

She treads across the hallway to the living room, fast before any of them follow her. She should've done that when Aline told her so. At least she'd avoid the legs that feel like spaghetti.

But the living room isn't empty. Two boys hugging each other are sitting on a torn couch with foam popping out of it. They startle and try to hide their faces.

"Does it look like I bite?" Néia says. "I won't ask you about Bhaskara."

"Sorry..." one of them mumbles, fluffs underneath his nose. "Sorry for what we did there."

Néia waves a hand and walks to the door. "You wouldn't scare a fly."

When she grabs the doorknob, she turns back to them.

"What are your names?"

"I'm Paulo." He grips his partner's legs. "He's Leo."

"Why are you working with Aline?"

"She... promised to smuggle a place for us in the white stars." The boy holds firmly his partner's thigh. Sweat beads on his fluffs like twinkling particles of salt. "She told us she'd send 100 people to the stars."

Néia nods. She wants to let it all sink in, but it's too much for her now.

She pries the door open without any other word and descends 3 flights of stairs. The building's old and ill-conserved, but has some areas completely overhauled. Hooks for drones and network routers line up on the ceiling, and she swears an elevator is dinging somewhere.

In the back of the building, Néia finds what used to be a kitchen: a rust-gnawed oven, a cracked sink, and an open refrigerator improvised as a cabinet for cleaning material. What grabs her attention, though, is a wide shelf set very high on one of the walls, even crossing the line—through a hole in the ceiling—of what once had been the floor of the upper story. A ladder had been put in a corner. Items for barges and motorboats are neatly positioned on the shelf: engines, sonars, control centers, life jackets, wax, and a ton of other stuff Néia doesn't even know how to name.

On the opposite wall, the one that connects the building to the outside, there's a wicket gate and what looks like a holder for some kind of weapon. A washed-out picture had been pasted next to it. It's Aline with another girl of about the same age. They're both smiling, pointing to the sky. Néia doesn't find much of her former student in the picture.

Néia finds a crack in the wall that works as a door to a solitary dock. This one had been fabricated primarily with PVC and later covered with a fall protection mat.

It is the end.

Néia stares between the two buildings framing the ocean, the ones from Aline's penthouse.

The water hardly ripples but for the pattering of the rain. A few meters ahead, boys and girls swim and dive from a canoe. Their giggles float in the air and remain suspended for an instant before fading. As if that place right on the edge of everything is making an effort to store their sound, knowing that laughter isn't as common around there.

Néia had met Aline in a flood. Everybody made friends in floods back then. They were both crammed inside a bus in the traffic jam—aka the best moment to have a nice talk with someone you don't know. Néia had lent Aline a notebook to fan herself because air conditioning systems in buses didn't last long when the money of public transportation leaked to the white stars that would supposedly save everyone. It was then Aline told her she wanted—*yearned* was the word—to enroll in a university. No matter the career, she'd told her, as long as she could buy a decent house far from the mess.

The kids row their canoe and tie it on a wooden pole on the dock, darting suspicious looks at the old woman sitting there, gazing at the intersection of ocean and city.

"Hey," one of them says, entering the building. A short black girl with cats on her bikini, barely the age Aline had been when she decided to study hard for the entrance exams. "The rain is picking up."

"I know. It's refreshing, though."

The girl shrugs and walks toward the abandoned kitchen. Néia stands and pulls her gently by the arm.

"What is the cosine of 60°?"

The girl opens her mouth, a curl of confusion on her lips. "I think it's one and a half."

Néis nods. "Aline taught you that."

"Yep." The girl muffles a laugh. "Don't know what this is used for, but she has those old notebooks of hers and says they're sacred."

They'd filled seven notebooks together. Exercises, mock exams, theory, and smiling faces next to correct answers. When the news reported about the successive shutting of the universities, Néia had finished proving two triangles congruent. That day, they ate leftovers from Christmas, and Néia told Aline she wouldn't stay. She had made a decision on the Slot Lottery after three months of thinking. Aline delicately tickled her eyelashes and thanked Néia for everything. Néia packed her stuff and left all her notebooks with Aline, including the blank ones. It had all been a little formal. Like a teacher leaving a classroom at the end of the semester, a mix of longing and professionalism in her chest. It was what they were, right? A teacher and a student.

They kissed each other's cheeks, hugged for longer than usual, and then nodded to each other. They were going to be fine. No one was dying. It was only a goodbye. Néia would leave to a distant place, but she'd work to visit Aline whenever she could.

"Do you like it here?" Néia asks the girl. The others now look at her with curiosity. "This city, the things Aline does for you..."

"I love here. But *Tia* says up there things last more."

They call her *tia*. Every child and teenager in Rio has a *tia*, no matter if she's blood-related or just a stranger they happen to meet along the way. Not a mother, not a teacher, or a friend. A *tia* is something else, an entity of its own. It's the glue that penetrates all the cracks of life and makes it resilient, even if just for a while.

"There you are." Aline stands in the kitchen, a puzzled

look on her face. She'd exchanged her clothes now that Néia had unmasked her. She wears a black tank top that exposes a tattoo on her right arm: the word "Remember" stylized with several spiraled edges. In all their calls, Néia had never noticed the tattoo. Aline always wore clothes that hid it. "Your baby girl has left."

"To where?" Néia enters the kitchen. The rain is picking up outside. By the height of the nautical shelf, the tide would probably rise soon.

"She thought you went back to her ship. Went after you saying she couldn't leave you alone and blah-blah-blah..."

"You had a gun, and you let her go."

"Didn't even have bullets."

"I need to get to her. Do you have a motorboat? Anything that travels fast."

"*Tia*, I think she knows how to handle herself."

"In a swimming pool, not here."

"A rainstorm is on the way, *tia*." She points at the skies. "Let that idiot go."

A hundred slots. One of them could've belonged to Aline, to the boys in love up there in the apartment, to that short girl that knows the cosine of 60°.

Black clouds whip off in bulks. A summer rainstorm is coming. It'd be quick and violent, as always.

"She's my responsibility." In a sense, she became Rebeca's *tia*. "She won't survive on her own."

Aline says nothing and ushers her to another dock, hid on yet another cracked wall, this time in a bathroom. The boat is a simple one. It has no cockpit, what means they won't be protected from the rain. It's crudely painted with flowers and mythological creatures scattering along the hull, swirled by signs of addition, subtraction, multiplication, and division. The boat's name is Arithmetic.

"She's using your chart," Néia says, touching the boat's control screen uninvited and opening Aline's chart. "She'll take the safest paths."

Aline initiates the boat and touches a set of pre-defined dots on the chart. She swivels to face Néia as the boat picks up speed.

"Tia, the floodstreets get really messy with hard rain. There's always accidents and—"

"Bla-bla-bla!" Néia opens and closes her fingers in front of Aline's face. "I didn't even have a canoe when I went back home with water up to my waist."

Aline opens her mouth to speak, but Néia stands in her stubborn pose. It had always worked with students: hands on the waist, squinted eyes, and a slightly scornful grin.

The storm picks up quickly, dust and water buffeting their faces. Of all the things that have changed down there, the unending cycle of heat and rainstorms isn't one of them. Aline's boat is rigged to go faster than its specs, so they drill through the rain as the day quickly darkens. Its algorithms make it swerve and shimmy to avoid the waves at the right time, preventing it from waterlogging.

Aline stands on the bow as if able to see through the storm veil. Néia tucks her hat on her pocket and grapples with the gunwale, her back spraining.

"We can't see anything!" Néia yells, then staggers to Aline's side.

"She's not far."

Aline fidgets in a bag and produces a cross-shaped drone. It swoops up from her hands. She turns on a cam feed on her pad, but it's hard to see anything but water spray.

"*Tia*, did you buy a new mattress?" Aline drapes an arm

over her shoulder.

"Now you're worried about my back pain."

"When I wasn't?"

"When you sent me to a dangerous building to search for you in a wrecked flat."

Aline snickers. "You must've met Valdir. I sent him there to report on you and plan ahead. He followed both of you for a while in the floodstreets. I wanted to make sure everything was all right."

"You what—"

"You must talk to the neighborhood's manager." Aline sways her head in a mocking tone.

Néia slaps the back of Aline's neck three times, water splashing off of it.

"*Tia!*"

"This is for being a liar. All those things you've been doing... with those people. You could've told me. Could've trusted me."

"I did a lot of bad stuff, *Tia*." Aline rubs her nape. "I'm not that bookish girl who wants to pass her entrance exams anymore. I'm in a gang. Not those young ones you saw there at the palace, no. That was just a play. But I... I have to do nasty things. To get money, to give drinking water to those boys in the building, to provide security so they can at least study in peace... People have no idea about the structure behind the things they glorify. It's not always a pretty structure."

Néia knows very well. Whenever someone in the Dandelion talks about the ingeniousness of a new hydromassage module—*it even has a panel to choose the bathtub's essence!*—Néia remembers the skeleton looming next to where Aline lived. She recalled the infernal noise, the toxic stench of annihilation and apocalypse, of millions of tons of iron and plastic and whatever being shifted day and night, corroding the communities all around.

The Arithmetic swerves on a tight floodstreet. The buildings' windows shine on both sides, too close to them. Even with the storm, Néia can see the silhouettes of people moving inside the apartments, maybe running to get their clothes off makeshift clotheslines, maybe leaving their homes temporarily—you always had to expect it's temporary—because they know the risks of collapse during storms.

"Remember," Néia says.

"What?" Aline doesn't take her eyes off the waters.

Néia puts a hand on Aline's tattoo.

"You never told me about it."

"Yep…" Aline says. "There's quite a while."

"Hey." Néia pulls the pad from Aline's hand and slides her hand over it to wipe the excess water. "There's something here. Wouldn't you say anything?" A white surface glints on the drone video feed.

Aline takes the pad back.

"That's a boat. I hadn't seen it."

"Let's go, then. It might be her."

Aline runs back to the control.

The Arithmetic skids through the water, swerving along obstacles that would be impossible to see with the naked eye. The boat leaves the tight floodstreet and accelerates through a larger one. Suddenly, Aline lowers the speed almost to a halt.

"What are you doing?" Néia yanks Aline's elbow, staring at the control screen. There's a label saying "Chemistry" on a dot not far ahead.

"We better get back," Aline says, her gaze faltering.

"Why?" Néia yells, a gust of dust and rain blowing on her face. "What is 'Chemistry'?"

But it's obvious. If there's an Arithmetic, of course, there are other, more challenging disciplines. The Chemistry approaches quickly, spilling water on the Arithmetic and halting right in front of it, blocking Aline's boat in a way that even its elaborate algorithms aren't capable of finding maneuverability solutions.

Aline sits down and sighs, closing her eyes. Not so surprised but stressed. The drone hands in front of her, and she pulls it down, almost throwing it sideways.

The Chemistry is a motorboat created especially for that new Rio. On the bow, a concave plaque of iron and aluminum, patched with wooden boards, works as a kind of shield. On the boat's sides, iron tweezers make it look like a big crab. Full of scratches, dents, and bullet holes, its hull sports a fading caricature of the agronomist Johanna Döbereiner.

But the problem is on the stern. A lady and a man armed with submachine guns.

"And you say I'm the one who doesn't know how to pick friends." Néia bites her lips. Those two aren't part of the Palace's play anymore.

"*Tia*, this is Tainá and Miguel," Aline says without standing or even looking at the cool-looking duo in the Chemistry. "This is my *Tia* Néia."

Tainá and Miguel nod curtly. Néia grunts in acknowledgment. Miguel runs his finger over the Chemistry's controls, and the two boats bump into each other. Miguel is a short, black man wearing wet glasses and a tank top of some soccer team invented down there after Néia left. Tainá wears a bulletproof vest over grey and shabby overalls. Her hair is blonde and shaggy, and she has a piercing on her nose. Both have the same tattoo Aline has on their left arm. *Remember.* Tainá is the girl from the abandoned kitchen picture. So she and Aline are at least friends enough to print a picture and hang it on the wall.

"Not sure if you noticed, but we're in a hurry," Néia says. "And you stuck this weird boat right on our way."

Tainá sticks a hand in her overalls' pocket and throws a cell phone to Aline. It drops on her feet. Aline finally stares at the duo.

"It was floating near the Lago do Machado," Miguel says. Néia is nervous, with her back hurting and her legs tired, but she muffles a laugh anyway. Lago do Machado—Machado's Lake—is the former Largo do Machado—Machado's Plaza. You only need to remove a letter when it floods.

"She must've dropped it," Aline says, grabbing the device. "We want to go on, folks. We're busy."

"Dropped?" Tainá snorts a laugh full of scorn. "You didn't hide it very well, Line. I think you don't remember so well." Tainá taps her tattoo.

"Give it to me." Néia pulls the cell phone from Aline's hand, scratching Aline's arm. She feels guilty for a moment, but then it quickly goes away. "What the hell is that?"

A padded cell phone with a floating case. On the screen, a green dot blinks, showing exactly where they are.

"You put it on the Boto…" Néia nods, slowly understanding the presence of those two right there. "You… You only let Rebeca go so she could be captured by these two bandits. Now I see the kind of person you became." Néia keeps nodding, mouth agape, water running down her cheeks.

Aline faces her with pinched lips. She opens her mouth but can't say anything. Typical of people who screwed up.

"It's our biggest opportunity, Line," Miguel says. "Jump over here, and let's go after that fool."

"Don't talk like that!" Néia yells at the young man, carefully stepping forward and pointing a finger to his face. They're close now with the boats touching each other. "You know her to speak about her like that?"

Néia swivels and points to Aline.

"And you! You played me for an idiot. Do you remember what I said when I waited for you for a lesson, and you had gone to a party? You lied, telling me you'd eaten spoiled chicken and couldn't come. Do you remember?"

Aline lowers her head and says: "You told me you wouldn't be played for a fool."

"Okay. Then you remember. And you did what you did now, even knowing that."

Tainá leaps to the Arithmetic.

"Since she arrived on Earth…" Tainá nods at Néia without breaking her gaze from Aline. An expression of disgust lines up on her lips. "You're erratic. You only talk about her, only think about her. You didn't even come to the meeting a few days ago. Where are your ideas now? Why bring seven more children and teenagers to the building last week? Only to deceive them with grammar classes that won't be useful for nothing in their lives?"

Néia inhales, wanting to interfere, to slap their faces. Of the three of them. She can't forget Miguel, gawking at the mess from the Chemistry. But everything that comes into her mind is Rebeca. Even with a useful map, it's not improbable that the girl is lost in the floodstreets and floodcenters of Rio, bouncing from one place to the other. And damn, how she draws attention with that shiny Boto and those expensive clothes and that arcologic girlish way. If she arrives safely at her ship, it will be like winning the lottery.

The longer Néia waits for that useless scuffle to end...

Aline cries. Tainá too, speaking between her teeth..

"...and it's not because I love you that I think you're being reasonable. Miguel and I are taking control from now on." She straightens the submachine gun in her right hand. Things are getting ugly.

"You don't..." Néia started.

Tainá raises the gun and points it to Néia, who slaps the barrel.

"Get this thing off my face!" she says. She's used to the boldness of those who carry fire guns. Sometimes, to enter Aline's community, she had to explain her business to milicianos and drug dealers. She had to tell them she was a teacher, and show them her papers, notebooks, and books while someone had a gun pointed at her. "Look, I—"

Aline punches Tainá's face.

"Not that..." Aline roars. "No, not that."

Néia steps back and slips on the Arithmetic's deck. A lancing pain goes through her back. She groans.

Aline jerks the submachine gun from Tainá's hand and throws it behind her, next to the Arithmetic's controls. Then, she lifts her partner and pushes her off the boat.

"Never point a gun at my *Tia*!" Aline screams in between her teeth, a rough, weakened voice.

Néia doesn't waste more time. She kneels and crawls to the controls, reactivating the Arithmetic's algorithms and setting them to an urgent priority. The boat jolts and lurches, quickly sliding through the waters, and leaving the Chemistry behind. Miguel yells and treads to the Chemistry's control.

Aline staggers and holds Néia firmly by the arms, placing

her on one of the boat's seats.

"Are you okay?" Aline asks, gasping.

"These slots are really something to you, aren't they?" Néia says, teeth clenched. Her back pain slowly recedes. Her knees are scraped, and she's still a bit winded.

Aline sits beside her, staring at the soaked deck. A tiny keychain tinkles in a corner: a heart enveloping Christ The Redeemer. It's something that Néia hadn't thought still existed, even a bit anachronistic. Must be vintage. Aline kneels and takes it. She bites her lips and presses the keychain tight in her hand.

"There's nothing more important than sending those kids and teenagers to the free slots up there," Aline says, recomposing her voice. "Not only Rebeca's slots. There are many others. Many thousands of slots were never allocated for hundreds of crazy and inhuman reasons. There's no space for everyone, I know, but there's space for a lot of people."

Néia nods. She agrees and even feels a bit disgusted to be working for Ferdinando's daughter, to be fighting and risking her own and Aline's lives to go after Rebeca and save her.

"You could've told me you were dating. Didn't need to push her off the boat. She wasn't going to shoot. If she likes you, she wouldn't do it. I know a serious threat from a fake one. She just wanted to impress you, to show you how she's all-in in this cause of yours."

"We're gonna fight so much..." Aline rubs her hands on her face as if it's possible to dry it. "But she'll understand. I pushed her because then I knew the Chemistry wouldn't follow us so quickly. Miguel will have to rescue her first. And she'll think twice before coming after us now. And before... pointing a gun at you."

"And you're gonna lose your place in your gang? And all the work you're doing to educate those young folks, giving them better conditions, and... planning their escape or whatever you prefer to call this madness?"

Aline shrugs.

"I'm the spark. They have enough to go on without me. I—I didn't want to involve you, Tia. But I did. I'm sorry."

The Arithmetic takes a turn and accelerates through a narrow floodstreet. Marquês de Paraná street, says a sign graffitied with green letters. Aline stands and sets the boat in rescue mode so it can look for accidents in the water. Flashlight drones buzz from a little box in the back. Perhaps one of those, from another boat, has already found Rebeca and now she's safe in a stinky dock drinking a cup of hot tea made with turvy water.

"Who will you remember?" Néia asks, looking at Aline. "Now you're going to tell me."

Aline frowns, fidgeting with Tainá's keychain in her hands.

"Our gang is called Remembrance. We've tried to go to the Dandelions once. Twelve gang members and seventeen people from ten to twenty-two years old. We knew about the slots, but we deemed it impossible to get hold of them through legal or illegal means. If we wanted to get in, we had to do it like... pirates. We stole one of the scientific cargo ships in a research station on the Caju Artificial Island. And then we went to space without planning too much." She twirls the keychain more intensely, her eyes lost and without focus. "We've coupled with one of the airlocks in the Dandelion #14. We've explained who we were, Earth refugees from Rio. We've talked with one of the directors. Nothing. We then tried Dandelions #13 and #12. No one allowed us in. Even knowing we had kids aboard. We even tried the Supraeuropean and the Canadian Dandelions, but no one let us in. We thought of using explosives that we had brought with us, but we couldn't risk it with the kids. Then we gave up. We had to come back. We didn't have enough resources to stay there for long, knocking from door to door like beggars."

You can't see tears in the rain, but Aline's eyes are red. Néia puts a hand over Aline's leg.

"If you don't want to talk about it…" Néia shakes her head.

"It's okay. Once in a while, it's really good to recall how everything was real. Tainá is right. Time goes on, and we forget the details. I don't want to forget anything. On our return trip, we had a problem with the cargo ship's propulsion system, which was already battered because we didn't have enough for maintenance. We entered the atmosphere without the proper protections in place, and some folks didn't even have how to fasten themselves to the seats during reentrance. We lost four members of our gang and three young ones. One of them was Isabele's brother. Isabele is that girl you were talking to at the dock."

Néia gulps. Sixty-three years old, and she thought it was unlikely for her to listen to a surprising story. She breathes in deeply. She'd lived with a husk around her for nine years. A white and rigid husk that now begins to crack.

"I've put the cell phone in Rebeca's boat," Aline says, standing and peeking at the controls. "To please Tainá and… to deceive myself. I've put it right in a place where Rebeca would see it. She must've realized what it was and threw it into the water."

The Arithmetic swerves into another floodstreet. The

drones gather at a specific point, lightning one region.

"We found something," Aline says.

Néia stands up quickly, her back aching. She leans on the gunwale and stares at the water, trying to identify something in the middle of the rain's haziness.

And she does.

"No..." Néia inhales, sucking a bit of rain.

A boat turned upside down, the drones bathing it in dull light.

"Is it hers?" Aline sets the Arithmetic to a halt.

"Yes." Néia would recognize that top-notch, unscathed hull anywhere. "I have to go."

"Go where?" Aline leaps from the controls and grabs Néia's shoulder.

"I told her I can dive." Néia stares at the turned boat, yearning to see someone around it, swimming, floating, waving for help... "It's my job."

"You're nuts."

She might as well be. People called her nuts when she crossed the city to teach math to someone she knew on a bus ride—and for 1/3 the price she usually charged. And she told herself she was mad when she entered a white-walled, glistening office and registered herself as a Dandelion citizen.

Aline anticipates what she's going to do. She pulls her blouse's sleeve, but Néia dodges her and throws herself into the water, ignoring the sudden exertion on her back.

There are things you only learn when you experience it yourself, no matter how many times people tell you what it's like. One of them is grief. When Joel, Clara, and Tintin died, Néia insisted to herself she wouldn't suffer for too long. It was illogical to suffer. They wouldn't come back, no matter how many tears she shed. All they would want was for her to keep on with her teachings and her samba. It was what she wanted too. And yet, she closed herself to the world for months, defying all logic she always swore was the core of her being.

Another thing you only know when you do it yourself is fighting desperately for any sliver of control you grasp over your life. You know you still can do something with that frazzled, moth-eaten thread. And that's when you dive. That's when logic dies, and 1/100 becomes 99/100 in your mind.

The Rio down there, the one she left behind, is murky but for the wavering silhouettes of buildings and the trash that drifts along.

She looks up. The boats had moved to somewhere on her left. No, not them. Her. It's a river down there, an ever-moving stream of water that feeds from the sea and rives itself to become the veins of Rio.

Rebeca's body floats a few meters from her, arms and legs dangling at the will of the currents.

Néia swims at it.

She thumps against a wall and grapples with a window sill, her nails breaking.

She can't be sucked in.

Propelling her feet against the wall, she thrusts herself and curls her arms around Rebeca's torso.

Her back twinges.

The stream takes hold of them and absorbs them into the window.

As the song says, a river passed through her life, and her heart had let itself be taken away.

The sun always shines after summer rainstorms. At times it

comes with a drizzle, at others, it accompanies a rainbow. Other times still, it just shines.

Maybe Néia decided to leave Earth because the sun hadn't risen from behind the clouds for many successive weeks. Maybe it was the ceaseless rain, or perhaps the waters inundating the shop where she bought breakfast on her way to Aline's house. It could've even been because one day when returning home on a canoe, she found the bar where she drank beer and sambaed completely wrecked.

Néia opens her eyes. The sun shines. No rain, no rainbow.

Her back still aches, but mildly, now it has already betrayed her.

She's on a dock, groggy, wrapped in coats and linens, laying still on disheveled quilts. Not as hard as wood, not as soft as a good quality mattress.

"Wake up, idiot!"

Aline is on another dock, on her knees, doing mouth-to-mouth resuscitation on Rebeca.

Néia is unable to say or do anything but weep. When was the last time she cried, anyway? It must've been due.

"Wake up, wake up!" Aline screams.

Rebeca coughs, spitting water, chest heaving up and down. Aline throws herself on her back, lying on the dock and staring up.

Néia could list another hundred reasons for going away, another bunch of unsatisfactory answers that would never please the part of her that searches for logic. But when she left Earth, she was tired. Exhausted from fleeing from the rising tide that one day would reach her neck. From living at the edge of probability, about to become a statistic. And that should suffice as an answer.

The Boto takes a turn into a floodstreet crammed with barges fully loaded with crates in front of a warehouse. The water breeze shoves the smell of fish at their faces. They're in Vila Isabel, where samba was born in Rio and never drowned. Small guitars sound frisky somewhere around the docks.

"We're looking for big crates marked with a black cross," Néia says. They've got the location of all five bronze eagles. A scavenger had taken them years ago but never sold or put them to any kind of use. "We won't be able to lift them on our own."

Rebeca types something on the Boto's control screen.

"Aline is already there with Paulo and Leo," Rebeca says, standing and gulping a sun-blocking pill. "Paulo said they're bringing a... crab?"

Néia smiles.

The Boto comes to a halt and thunks on a barge. Aline is climbing one of the boxes, one with a big black cross scrawled on it. Paulo and Leo are behind her, adjusting harnesses and attaching them to the boxes.

"They're in good shape," Aline says, jumping into the Boto. "Oxidized and dirty, but nothing that a good wash won't solve."

"All right." Rebeca grabs her pad and opens Ferdinando's to-do list. Her eyes are wet, and her fingers hover above the pad, not checking the relics she has just found.

In the floodstreet, the Chemistry approaches with its flashy pincers, its bow so patched that it looks like a checkered shirt for a June Party. Rebeca touches the controls to move the Boto. Miguel fumbles with some levers that position the Chemistry's pincers toward one of the boxes. Tainá doesn't even glance at Aline.

"It's a long way to your ship," Néia says. "We have to be careful."

Rebeca shakes her head slowly, then turns to Néia and Aline. "You both know Rio better than I do. Find a good place for them."

"But our arrangement..." Aline's mouth hangs open. It's the first time Néia hears anything about a deal between them. "I help you find your stuff, you free up slots for my students."

Néia gapes at them, dumbfounded. Indeed, they both spent over an hour together on the dock after the rescue, while Néia had fallen into a deep sleep and dreamt of Joel and Tintin eating fried cod balls in a restaurant floating above the clouds. She doesn't usually remember her dreams, even less when they feature her husband and her dog, but that one had left a pleasant aftertaste, just like... Well, like fried cod balls sprinkled with olive oil.

"Our deal is up," Rebeca says. "I already registered Paulo and Leo to go and release all remaining slots. Just tell me any name you want."

The boys exchange looks, bewildered, then yell and embrace each other, jumping and making the barge sway.

"Hey, hey, hey!" Aline laughs. "If you throw those eagles on the water, you won't go anywhere until you get them back."

Néia approaches and pats Rebeca's elbow. Her lips form the question she wants to ask, whether Rebeca filled up a slot for Aline already. But the answer's in the way Aline looks at Paulo and Leo, in the way she always dismissed Néia when they talked about registering Aline for the Slot Lottery that opened every month since the Dandelions lift-off. In the picture with Tainá in that abandoned kitchen. In the little

Christ the Redeemer keychain with the keys to some room they both share.

"Both of you." Néia points to Aline and Rebeca. "And you too." Then to Paulo, Leo, Miguel, and Tainá. "I'm in Vila Isabel, and there's a floodcenter back there blistering with rodas de samba and beer at 4 °C. So now we oughta go back and have some good time."

They all look at each other and smile. Paulo and Leo leap into the Boto. Aline walks to the Chemistry and hands the keychain to her partner. Tainá tries to grab it from her hand, but Aline holds it and squeezes her fingers. They both exchange a brief look, the kind Néia knows very well, meaning the sun will rise after the rainstorm.

"Won't you mark your father's items?" Néia asks Rebeca when the Boto starts.

Rebeca's mouth tightens. She slides her finger up and down Ferdinando's to-do list. She doesn't check anything.

"One of the things my father told me after Mom was kidnapped..." she says, almost to a murmur so only Néia would listen. "Actually, one of the last things before I thought I was adult enough not to sit with him every night. He told me the job he regretted the most in his life was taking the Christ to a Dandelion."

"So he realized it was kind of overkill?" Néia nods, partially answering her own question.

"It's not that." Rebeca shakes her head, her finger still rolling down the list. "He said the was happy to preserve a statue so important for the country and the world. But he told me many people who lived here had helped him. A lot of folks volunteered. So many people believed in the task of saving that statue."

"But..." Néia knows pretty well the adversative conjunctions that are part of life when you live enough. They often precede a list of regrets.

"He had nightmares with the people that helped him. He dreamed of them drowning down here. He wanted to know where each one of them was and even tried to go after them once in a while... But he never saw most of them ever again."

Néia squeezes Rebeca's hand. She also had nightmares about the people down there, and they normally involved water and sun.

"I can make other lists," Rebeca says, assenting, more decisiveness on her face than before. Actually, Néia hadn't seen her with that optimistic sparkle in her eyes yet. "Lists that regard other things left behind down here." She glances at Paulo, Leo, and Aline.

The Boto vibrates through the floodstreets and ends in a floodcenter with the Chemistry right behind.

Néia sits, stretching her back. Aline sits by her side, drapes an arm over her shoulder, and kisses her cheek. Without glimmering avatars, without the false formality of goodbyes. Anyway, Néia isn't a teacher anymore. Aline is even more of a teacher than her, nowadays. Néia is only a *tia*.

Rebeca sits in front of Aline. She stares at her with a dour look. For a moment, Néia thinks they're going to start a fight.

"Is there karaoke around here?" Rebeca asks.

Aline nods. "There are two in the Floodcenter September 28th."

"There's a secondhand bookshop there as well," Néia adds, pointing to a triangle on their map. "We might find that book you want there."

The Boto accelerates and arrives at the September 28th Floodcenter.

The last time Néia cried before waking up on the dock was in her Dandelion's quarters, lights off, a troubled Earth static outside her round window. She'd asked herself, even whispered in the dark, alone, if she would die before ever feeling she made any right decisions in her life.

But now, while the Boto weaves its way across the veins of Rio, toward the floodcenter and the samba, she's 99.99999 9% sure she'd just made one.

About the Author

Renan Bernardo is a Brazilian writer of science fiction and fantasy from Rio de Janeiro.

His work has been published in English, Portuguese, German, Japanese, and Italian. He's also a SFWA member.

You can find his stories in several publications including *Apex Magazine, Podcastle, Escape Pod, Solarpunk Magazine, Dark Matter Magazine, Translunar Travelers Lounge,* and *Daily Science Fiction.* His story, "The Plasticity of Being," is forthcoming at *Tor.com (Reactor).*

His writing scope is broad, from secondary world fantasy to dark science fiction, but he enjoys the intersection of climate narratives with science, technology, and the human relations inherent to it. History, science, and music are others of his passions.

He lives in Rio de Janeiro, but you can find him in the digital world at Twitter (@RenanBernardo) or BlueSky (@renanbernardo.bsky.social).

More From Android Press

<u>ANTHOLOGIES</u>
Bioluminescent: A Lunarpunk Anthology
ed. Justine Norton-Kertson

2022 Best of Utopian Speculative Fiction
ed. Justine Norton-Kertson

Mothersound: The Sauútiverse Anthology
ed. Wole Talabi

Fighting for the Future: Cyberpunk and Solarpunk Tales
ed. Phoebe Wagner

Voodoonauts Presents: (Re)Living Mythology
ed. Yvette Lisa Ndlovu, Shingai Njeri Kagunda, H.D
. Hunter, L.P. Kindred

<u>COLLECTIONS</u>
Caged Ocean Dub: Glints & Stories
by Dare Segun Falowo

rivers in your skin, sirens in your hair
by Marisca Pichette

<u>GRAPHIC NOVELS</u>
Anticipation of Hollowness
by Renan Bernardo, Michele Paris, and Lorenzo Livrieri

Razor's Edge
by Phil Emery and Toeken

<u>GAMES</u>

Ninefox Gambit RPG
by Yoon Ha Lee

Fight for the Future: A Cyberpunk-Solarpunk RPG
by Justine Norton-Kertson